curious little WEREW🐾LF

KATIE SALIDAS

Cover Art by
https://www.wegotyoucoveredbookdesign.com/

Published by:
Rising Sign Books
http://www.KatieSalidas.com

For more information about my books email:
katiesalidas@gmail.com

Things would be perfect if supernatural disasters would quit creeping up and ruining Giselle's happy new life.

After finally finding the fur-ever home she's always wanted a witch blows into town promising to reveal the bloody past of Giselle's birth, and the circumstances that led the little werewolf to end up in the foster care system to begin with.

Hot on the witch's trail, another pack of wolves is on the hunt for revenge, and will accept nothing less than her death in retribution for the havoc she's wrought on them.

Caught in the crossfire, Giselle desires only the truth, and if the witch is who she claims to be, the little werewolf must protect her at any cost. If she's lying, though, Giselle risks her own kind seeing her as a traitor. Neither her new pack nor her hottie witch boyfriend Damien can offer any help. Giselle is on her own again. And if she makes the wrong decision, she'll lose the only link she has to her own past.

Titles By Katie Salidas

Chronicles of the Uprising
Dissension
Complication
Revolution
Transition
Retribution
Annihilation

Little Werewolf
Pretty Little Werewolf
Curious Little Werewolf

Immortalis
Carpe Noctem
Hunters & Prey
Pandora's Box
Soustone

Immortalis Companions
Moonlight
Dark Salvation

Be sure to stop by KatieSalidas.com and sign up
to the Paranormal Posse Newsletter.
All new subscribers will be sent a FREE ebook.

Autographed Editions of all Katie Salidas books
may be purchased at
www.KatieSalidas.com

1

"That's it. It's all over." Giselle picked at a slice of pepperoni on her meat lover's pizza, wishing she could scarf down the greasy goodness, but depression had turned her stomach against her. She sighed like a woman on death row, knowing the end was near. Arguably, the more rational side of her mind knew better, but that voice of reason was so small it could hardly be heard over the packed restaurant. In the booth next to her sat a rowdy bunch what appeared to be freshmen. They had no clue what was in store for them. Tomorrow would change their lives entirely. But tonight that wouldn't suppress their wild hoots and hollers about how cool they were going to be. Bunch of kids, *just like her,* if she'd let go of the angst. Frustration had angry words teetering on the edge of her tongue. Giselle wanted to make a snide comment, but before she opened her mouth, reason won out, and she realized it was her own annoyance rather than the rowdy boys next to her that was more bothersome.

Sammy's was the most popular pizza joint in town, but this evening saw it packed tighter than her sister Taylor's shoe closet. By her count, half the population of her school and maybe some from neighboring ones were there, along with families and more small children than her poor ears could handle.

Kids were loud... too loud. The screeching and laughter had her wolf retreating to the farthest reaches of her mind for peace. Noise drowned out nearly all other sounds, making it hard for her to concentrate on her own table and hear the footsteps of her date as he returned.

Forty-five minutes Giselle and Damien had waited for a table to become available. Forty-five minutes of pure hell. And then to top that off, it had taken an additional thirty ear-splitting minutes of listening to others enjoying their pizza before her own had arrived.

Operating purely on hunger, Giselle had wolfed down half the pizza so quickly she'd barely even tasted it, and that's when the depression struck her. This was the last pizza she'd eat as a free woman. After tonight, it would be the institutionalized meals filled with taking turns talking about her day and minding proper manners. Not to mention the whole food, organic, homogenized, non-GMO, tasteless, soul-less cooking she'd be subjected to. Her wolf still salivated at the thought of more meat, but the human side of her warred with an anxious stomach. And now all that remained was a single slice.

"Oh, don't look so sad, Elle." Damien returned to their table bringing an invisible cloud of soap and a bit too much cologne with him. At least he didn't smell as bad as some boys her age, though he could cut back on the body spray. Human girls weren't as sensitive to the nasal burning that followed a fresh application of manly smell, but she was no human, and her eyes were beginning to water from the fumes. He took his seat and reached across the table, fingers dangerously close to that last slice of pizza.

She was sure he'd been trying to hold her hand, but the wolf in her was agitated, and possessive. Involuntarily, Giselle let out a little growl.

"I will never understand your mood swings," Damien sighed. He pulled back his hand and busied himself with the salt shaker instead.

"Sorry. I'm in a funk. Not ready for summer to be over." She glanced around, noting similar disillusioned looks on other faces belonging to upperclassmen like herself. Tomorrow would be the first day of another school year, and there was no getting out of it. The summer had been so much fun. She'd celebrated her official adoption and been welcomed into the pack with open arms. They'd spent every free moment swimming, shopping, and hiking, and the moonlight runs... pure heaven. Her wolf lived for those. Total freedom to wander the desert, chasing jackrabbits, and the invigorating feeling of the warm breeze rushing through her fur. Some days, the best part of being a wolf was the shedding of her human skin and letting the animal take the lead. As a wolf, her senses were stronger. She relied much more on instinct and feeling.

Lost in the daydream of exchanging her clothes for a fur coat and breaking into a full run in the soft desert sand was enough to have her wolf rising to the surface, whimpering for one last run before rules and order demanded she adhere to curfews again.

The weight of the human world became secondary when she was a wolf, as if it were only a dream. She didn't even need to run with her pack to enjoy herself, unlike other wolves. Being alone only heightened the sensation of pure freedom. But she was a lone wolf no longer. She had a pack – one that she'd never dreamed she find. And even with their quirks and rules, she was coming to the realization that with them was where she belonged.

Even Damien, supernatural in his own right, could never appreciate that true sense of freedom. Giselle wondered if there were some kind of witch equivalent, she but doubted it. Witches seemed stricter in their rituals and ceremonies than even some religious humans she'd met over the years. Magic was not fun; it was something to work at. Duty and service, those Damien seemed to understand, and Giselle was certainly learning it too, being in a pack. Duty and service were the opposite of freedom in every way, and that sobering thought brought her back to reality.

She let out another loud sigh and turned away from the last slice of pizza staring her down, begging to be eaten.

Martina would be proud. Her new mom was constantly harping on her about her diet, even more so in recent months since she'd joined the whole plant-based foods movement. If it weren't for the fact that wolves needed meat, she'd have sworn Martina would have made them all go vegan. A shudder ran through her body, sending her wolf retreating to the farthest depths of her mind at that horrid thought.

Martina's voice whispered in the back of her mind: *Good little wolves eat more than just junk food, dear. You need lots of lean meat – and veggies, too!*

Despite the desire to eat a half-pound burger just to spite Martina's new diet regime, she couldn't have asked for a better mom. She'd never truly had one of those before. Foster moms were nice, until they found out about her condition. Martina had been the first to truly accept her and even love her for what she was. Still, though, at times her thoughts wandered to her own mother. She had to be out there, somewhere.

Questions like that lead her down a dark path of anxiety coupled with feelings of abandonment she'd rather not deal with. The foster life was not real life; just an endless stream of heartbreaking loss. Not something she'd wish on her worst enemy. Being tossed from one home to another, never a good fit for any family because of her... condition.

"If you don't snap out of this funk, I'll work my magical mumbo-jumbo on you." Damien wiggled his fingers and winked.

That smile of his was magic enough. He never failed to charm her with it, and this time was no different.

"You act like it's the end of the world, not the end of summer." Those magic fingers of his tiptoed their way toward the remaining slice of pizza.

She'd already snapped at him once, so she let him feel he stole it. "Might as well be the end of the world." Giselle pouted. "My schedule arrived last week. I got Mr. Harper again. You know that guy has it in for me."

Damien drew in his breath. "Eww, sorry."

"Yeah. I had to take another lab credit for my transcripts, so Chem 2 was my best option. Harper barely passed me last year. I swear he tried to find every reason to take off points in my labs. That man hates me. But he's the only chemistry teacher."

"You couldn't take physics or life science?"

"*If* I pass Chem 2 this year, I'll take physics senior year. That's what the career counselor said."

Damien swiped the last slice of pizza off the pan before Giselle could mutilate it further and shoved it into his mouth.

"Hey!" She playfully snarled at him.

He chewed his bite quickly and winked at her. "You weren't eating it. Just peeling off meat chunks."

"Hyena," Giselle teased him.

Damien shrugged. "As long as I get a slice or two, call me what you will."

"Speaking of scavengers" – Giselle nodded to the two girls walking through the front door – "Here come my sisters. Cunning little wolves. They waited just long enough to join us in the kill."

"What?" Damien choked on a pepperoni.

"Well, they knew I'd be here and that Sammy's would be packed. Now they don't have to wait for a table." If she'd been smarter, Giselle might have tried the same thing.

Taylor and Di sauntered up, all smiles, and scooted right into the booth as if they'd been invited.

"Thanks for saving us a seat, Elle," Di said. She tucked her Grey hobo bag in between herself and Giselle, and then picked up a menu. "Are we ready to order?"

Giselle snickered. "How long did you hang back at the house before deciding Damien and I had had enough alone time?"

Taylor stashed her own purse and pulled out her lipstick and mirror. "Oh, no. We weren't waiting. We went shopping. Di needed a new back-to-school outfit."

"Because the one you bought last week wasn't trendy enough?" Giselle asked.

"Well, I heard that Cynthia Struthers is planning on wearing a canary yellow romper. The one we spotted at the mall last week. It had the cutest ties at the hem of the shorts and that really deep V-neck. Pairs perfectly with those white rope wedges. Anyway..."

Giselle's mind wandered as soon as Di and Taylor started talking clothes. Fashion was one thing. She enjoyed looking her best, but Di and Taylor made a career of being on top of all the latest trends, and she could hardly keep up. The last time she'd worn a romper, she was probably still in diapers, and now they were the latest trend, especially in blinding colors like yellow and hot pink. Not something she'd be caught dead in. But she'd never say that out loud. Smiling and nodding, she let Di go on about having to make a statement on the first day of school. It wasn't until their blank stares had landed on Giselle that she realized she'd been asked a question.

"Uh... Whatever, right?" The standard catch-all reply usually worked, accompanied by a smile and shrug when Giselle didn't know the question.

Taylor huffed in response. "Honestly, Elle. You know I live and breathe fashion. Just let me pick out your outfit, okay?"

Happy to not have to do anything, and at the same time to avoid an argument with her sisters, Giselle nodded eagerly. "Sure. Make me beautiful."

"Ah. That's my department," Di said. "I'm thinking we go with an updo for you. Nothing severe, but we'll get your hair out of your face and do a little contouring on those cheeks."

Damien chucked.

"Keep laughing, witch, and I'll send them over to your house for a little manscaping." Giselle narrowed her eyes wickedly at him, half considering the option. It would make for a fun video to post on her profile. She'd get a million hits for sure.

Damien held his hands up in surrender. "No, thanks. I'm good here. I'm happy to silently bask in the glory of having three gorgeous girls at my table and the entire restaurant jealous of me."

Giselle laughed. "Who's jealous?"

Damien looked around the room, and his eyebrow quirked up. "Well, those people are, for sure. They've been staring at us since we came in here."

Giselle looked in the direction he indicated. Two guys she'd never seen before were looking at them, but as soon as Giselle spotted them, they turned their heads away, toward a woman approaching their table. "Nah, they're just waiting for their mommy to get back from the bathroom."

Damien looked back and then did a double take.

"What's the matter?" Giselle asked, catching the odd way he'd straightened up in his seat.

"Nothing."

"Don't lie to me. I can smell a lie, remember?"

"You can't smell a lie," he said.

"Maybe not literally, but I can hear the uptick in your heart and the sudden whiff of deodorant. You're sweating now... You're busted. 'Fess up! You know them?"

Damien looked back again, his brow furrowing giving age to his features. "No. But I recognize the pendant that woman is wearing. She's a witch, but not my coven."

"This is Vegas, remember? Tourist town," Taylor said, as if he needed the reminder.

"And I'd be okay with that if we were closer to the strip. But..." Damien's words trailed off. He reached for his phone and sent a quick text. "You know how it is... Supes all have to check in."

Giselle rolled her eyes. "Momma has you trained well."

"It's all fun and games until a war breaks out," Damien defended.

"Can we order already? I'm starving," Di said, setting her menu heavily on the table.

"Good luck grabbing a waiter. Our drinks have been empty for hours." Damien tilted his ice-less empty cup for effect.

"Shut up. We haven't even been her for hours," Giselle said. She stood and grabbed hold of the nearest guy in a white shirt and apron. "Find our waiter.... please."

Looking something between shocked and annoyed, the guy eased out of her grip and nodded.

"Want to tone down the Alpha a bit, Elle? We don't want anyone spitting in our food," Taylor said.

"That's the thanks I get for trying to help." Giselle sat back down in the booth.

"Thanks, sis," Di said with a smirk.

Damien's eyes drifted back over to the two guys and the lady sitting with them. Giselle caught his distraction and wanted to press the issue, but thought better about it. Wolf business was enough stress; she didn't really want to add in witch politics on top of that. And she would have left it there, except for the fact that the woman not only met her eye when she caught Giselle looking but held her gaze as if challenging her for dominance.

Witches don't do that.

Giselle's wolf rose to the surface, instinctively ready to meet that challenge. She curled her fingers, her nails elongating and sharpening into claws.

Long fiery red hair, a speckling of freckles across her nose, and the deepest green eyes she'd ever seen… if Giselle's wolf weren't already on the edge of surfacing, she might have picked up on the resemblance and the glimmer of familiarity there. But she was too far gone; her wolf, an Alpha, could not back down from this challenge.

The dominance game lasted long enough for others to notice, but just before Giselle took to her feet and added words to the tension, the woman smiled, nodded, and then turned away. Not a defeat by any stretch of the imagination; she'd gotten the better of Giselle, and that cocky smile proved it.

When Giselle had returned to her senses, she noticed how close to a change she'd come. Hairs on her arms and hands had bristled, and her nails sharpened into claws. She quickly hid them under the table and met the shocked expressions of her friends.

"Wanna tell me what that was all about?" Taylor asked.

Giselle looked to Damien. "I need to know who that woman is."

Damien nodded. All humor had left his face, replaced with pure fear. "Yeah," he practically choked on the words. "I'll find out."

2

That woman kept staring.

If she hadn't been with friends and in an over-stuffed restaurant, she might have made a scene of asking the lady what her problem was. But reason won over her animal instincts and Giselle walked calmly outside with Di and Taylor when they'd finished their food.

"So much for our last meal out, Elle. If you're going to wolf out every time some strange person looks at you, we're not taking you with us any-where." Taylor slung her bag over her shoulder and sauntered towards the car.

"Why was she staring so hard? That's what I want to know." Elle couldn't understand how they could be so calm about it. Life as a wolf was a far cry from normal, and when something went beyond their odd sense of normalcy, it usually wasn't good.

"Damien said he'd check it out. Just let it go for now. We have more important things to do tonight." Di slid into the driver's seat and checked her lip-stick in the mirror.

"Like what? Decide our outfits?"

"Don't be bitchy," Di said. "We need some rest. Tomorrow is an early day."

Yeah, right. Like sleep would come now. Giselle would be running the scene through her head all night at this rate. "Enjoy your beauty rest," she sighed.

"I will. And if you don't settle down, I'll tell Gavin to brew his famous sleepy time tea. That'll knock you out for sure." Di giggled. She pulled the car out of the parking lot and headed for home.

"Actually, that might not be a bad idea," Giselle said. Her mind would run for hours if she let it, and bitchy or not, Di was right – they needed to sleep for any hope of being alive for school in the morning.

"Well, I call first dibs on the bathroom," Taylor said.

"Just don't use up all the hot water this time." Giselle snickered at the way their lives could swing from supernatural to completely mundane in the span of a few minutes. All the problems in the world were small when it came to whether or not you got a hot shower.

"No promises. I have a brand new body wash I am dying to try." Taylor looked back and smirked.

"And you won't mind me stealing it when you're done." Giselle responded by sticking her tongue out.

Di put the car in park and hopped out first, grabbing a fistful of shopping bags from the trunk of the car.

She and Taylor were Olympic-level shoppers. Poor Gavin should have known better than to let them borrow his card. But the big softie that he was, he always made sure they and Giselle too were happy. She could never have dreamed of a better father. Giselle smiled inwardly, knowing that, despite the earlier grumpiness, there would be a fashion show in their room this evening as the frantic last minute wardrobe selections were made.

"How many outfits did you buy?" Giselle asked.

Di slammed the trunk of the car and held them proudly. "Just a few. I'll show you."

"She wants to make an impression." Taylor reached out and took hold of a few of Di's bags. "I've got a little something in here too."

"Can't wait to see." Giselle realized a moment too late that her tone had not quite conveyed the excitement the girls would expect. She hadn't intended to sound so glum, but before she could throw a perky wink or smile Taylor's way, her sister's expression soured.

"Why are you so down tonight? It can't just be the crazy lady who wigged you out. Is something going on with you and Damien?" Taylor asked as they walked up the driveway towards home. "We didn't seriously ruin your dinner, did we?"

"Why would you ask that?" Giselle wondered aloud. Had she given some impression that they were fighting? She had sounded a little grumpier than normal when she told him to check on that crazy woman, but she was two seconds away from wolfing out. Surely they had to understand how hard it was to speak lightly when the wolf was clawing its way to the surface.

Taylor shrugged. "You did seem a little grumpy towards him at dinner."

She wasn't... really. But the fact they'd crashed dinner was a little irksome. Perhaps that was part of her bitchy vibe. "Well, that does happen when your sisters decide to invite themselves on a date."

Di unlocked the front door. "Oh, so anytime you are with Damien now, it's considered a date?"

"Is it too much to ask to have a little alone time with my boyfriend every now and again?" Giselle lied. Her sisters were always underfoot; in a way, she enjoyed it, but using this as a distraction to the thoughts really troubling her was much better than divulging the truth. She wasn't really mad at either of them, but that woman and the strange familiarity about her flashed through Giselle's mind again. She saw again the way those green eyes had tried to bore straight into hers with that Alpha-like stare. But she was no wolf. Why would she do that? That was it. That woman had set her off. Who was she?

"You know, I knew him first." Di's snarky response brought Giselle back up from the darkness in her mind.

"And I am still dying to know what the big secret is between you two," Giselle responded.

"Never. Telling." Di looked Giselle straight in the eyes as she spoke, then smiled as if to punctuate the tease.

"Oh, I'll get it out of you one of these days," Giselle smirked.

"Not this again. Elle, drop it." Taylor groaned.

"Fine, we'll drop the subject of Damien all together. Let's talk about you and Ash. Planning to be his study buddy again this year?" Giselle asked Taylor.

Taylor sighed and rolled her eyes. She sped through the door and up the stairs before Giselle could get another word in.

"Something I said?" Giselle asked, when Taylor was out of sight.

"You're in rare form this evening, Elle," Di said. She tossed her purse and bags on the love seat as she passed through the living room on to the kitchen.

"Last day of freedom," Giselle sighed.

"I don't think so. Junior year is going to be great. I'm looking forward to getting back into it." Di poured herself a soda and grabbed a bag of chips.

"Didn't you have enough pizza to eat?" Giselle laughed, watching DI stuff a handful of chips into her mouth.

"Yeah, but I am craving carbs so badly right now." She stuffed another handful of chips into her mouth, and Giselle laughed at the irony. She was the one normally being scolded for her diet. Nice to see the shoe on the other foot.

"Looks to me like you're just as worried about the new school year as I am. Or do you regularly stuff your face when no one is looking?"

"Oh, all right. The pressure is on. It's been nice not to worry about my GPA for the last three months."

"Glad I'm not the only one. And you know I have Harper, first thing in the morning... Chem 2."

Di laughed, sending crumbs all over the kitchen counter. "Sorry, lady."

"Yeah. Not who I want to deal with... especially before caffeine has kicked in."

"We'll make a special stop on the way in tomorrow. I have a feeling we'll all need it."

Giselle nodded, then angled her head up to the ceiling. "Wanna tell me why Tay got all weird when I mentioned Ash? I thought they were getting close?"

"They were, and then suddenly stopped. She won't talk about it."

"You don't think Ash did anything, did he?"

"Nah. He's still an ass, but not a bad guy," Di said between bites.

Asher was more than just another wolf. Giselle herself had gotten lost in the pull of his gorgeous eyes, and if things had worked out differently, she might have been calling the hottie wolf hers. But she'd shoved aside the feelings she'd harbored for him when her sister had taken a real interest in becoming his girl. If something had happened between them, she needed to know. Sisters before misters, and all that. No matter what feelings she had buried for the wolfman, if he'd hurt her sister, she'd make him pay. "I'll find out. Leave it to me."

Di slugged her glass of soda and set it in the sink. "It will all come out eventually. No one can keep a secret in high school."

"Well, you and Damien apparently can." Giselle narrowed her eyes at Di.

"We agreed to change that subject."

"Sorry. Couldn't help it."

"And no... I'm still not telling." Di brushed past her and headed up the stairs. "And please don't ask again. Magical contract... remember?"

Damn that whole doctor-patient confidentiality thing the witches had going. Not knowing a secret was just eating away at her. It was probably nothing, too, but the not knowing part had her all twitchy. Something had happened between her sister and Damien, her boyfriend.

"Are you coming up? Time to pick outfits!" Di called from the top of the stairs.

3

Giselle cursed the siren screeching its serenade at god-awful-early-in-the-morning-o'clock and stumbled over to the alarm, nearly demolishing it with a slam of her fist on the snooze button. The sun had not yet pierced their window, but still she had to be up and mobile, pretending to be human. The first day of school demanded things like wearing clothes and keeping your eyes open, neither of which Giselle had any interest in at this early hour. But before she could turn and collapse back on her bunk, Taylor flicked on the light, blinding everyone with the power of three 60-watt bulbs. Might as was have been the sun for as bright as their room became in that blink of time.

"Warn a girl before you do that," Giselle hissed, covering her eyes against the sharp light.

"Have you gone vampire on us?" Taylor laughed.

"That's how we're starting today?" Di asked with a groan as she pulled herself upright. "Bitching at each other?"

"I'm not responsible for anything that comes out of my mouth before I've had coffee," Giselle grumbled, and went to work finding her assigned outfit for the day.

"Then just keep your mouth closed," Taylor said, with a surprising measure of snark.

A spiteful retort tiptoed to the edge of Giselle's tongue, but before it came out and ruined the day, she was able to rein it in, deciding that silence was better than picking a fight. She'd have plenty of time for that later, and all her uncaffeinated brain-power was needed to stop herself from falling flat on her face as she clumsily navigated stepping into her jeans. How anyone could be expected to function and learn at this ungodly hour of the day was beyond Giselle. Two, maybe three more hours of sleep, and she'd be just fine to start the day. Hell, she might not even need to drown herself in coffee to stay awake in first period. But no. Force kids to get up at the butt-crack of dawn and make them sit through boring lectures when they could barely keep their eyes open from exhaustion. That made sense.

Giselle grumbled to herself as she dressed, put on her makeup, and shouldered her backpack. She lumbered toward the car like a zombie in serious need of brains and contemplated how much sleep she could get between here and school.

Di and Taylor didn't seem to have as much problem with the morning as she. And as always, they managed to look like runway models as they strutted out to the car. *Bitches.*

"I know just what you need," Di, said as she started the engine. "A little vitamin C."

"Orange juice ain't going to help." The thought of it turned Giselle's stomach.

"Not that kind of Vitamin C," Di giggled. "You'll see." She pulled out of the driveway so fast she sent Giselle sideways in the back seat, nearly smashing her head against the window.

"In a hurry?" Giselle pulled her seatbelt taut and grabbed the oh-shit handle in the back, in case Di decided to pull any maneuvers like that again.

"Sorry. Just anxious," Di said sheepishly.

"Your outfit is fine." Giselle turned to look out the window. The sun was just starting to come up over the mountains. If she'd been in a better mood, she might have found it pretty the way the sky lightened from inky black to an almost light-steel-colored blue. Streams of early light escaped between mountain peaks, spotlighting the desert below, while above, gentle wispy clouds picked up the early light like streaks of highlighter outlining the sky. Mornings could truly be beautiful under the right circumstances; but early as it was, and on her way to school where she was expected to be more than just awake, her primitive brain would only be happy with one thing. And as if on cue, Di turned the car down a familiar road, and she saw ahead her salvation.

"Coffee," Giselle groaned as Di pulled up to the drive-through window.

"What kind?" Di asked.

"Espresso, straight up. Triple shot," Giselle said. "Stupid early bird classes," she grumbled.

"That'll burn a hole through your stomach. No," Di scoffed. She turned her head out of the window and ordered: "Two triple caramel lattes, no whip, extra foam, and an extra shot of caramel, please."

"So, and ulcer is bad, but diabetes is okay... gotcha!" Taylor snickered from the passenger seat.

"And one small skinny latte with a shot of vanilla, for Miss Priss." Di finished her order.

"I'm just saying, that's a whole lot of caffeine and sugar on an empty stomach," Taylor added.

"Uh, can I add three bagels and sides of cream cheese?" Di spoke again into the speaker box.

The reply came out somewhat garbled, but it sounded like they had the order right. Giselle couldn't care less about the sugar content at this point. The sun had barely come up over the mountains, and she was in no fit state to start the first day of her junior year. When the hot beverage came, it was all she could do not to guzzle it down in one slug.

Ten minutes later and freshly caffeinated, Giselle walked to her locker and began the ritual of organizing and finding the items she needed to start the day.

Asher came up behind her; the smell of him gave him away before he had the chance to startle her.

"Hey," she said lazily, as she continued to sort her binder and hunt for her favorite set of highlighters.

"Who you have first?" He leaned up against the locker next to hers. Giselle's eyes wandered of their own accord to his shirt, pulled tight across his muscular frame. It had to be the wolf in him that always aroused her attention, because her wolf was always close to the surface when he was near. Animal attraction was hard to overcome even when her rational mind knew he was off limits. She had a boyfriend, and Asher was supposed to be getting closer to Taylor. But still she had to look and appreciate the way his clothes showed off his natural physique.

"Harper." She tried to sound casual, as if she were just tired and had not been silently admiring him for the last thirty seconds. "You know. Because life couldn't be more unfair."

"Lucky for you, I have him too. Let's be lab partners again." Asher offered her one of his award-winning smiles to go along with his tempting offer.

"You think that's wise, after last year?" Giselle laughed and playfully smacked at his arm.

Asher deflected her swing and used her out-stretched hand to pull her in for a hug. "Oh, don't be such a pessimist. He loves us."

"He loves *you*." She pushed away from his body. "For what reason I can't say, but not me."

Asher laughed. "Just be a good little wolf and do as you're told. He likes rule followers."

"I don't have near enough caffeine in me this morning to come up with an appropriate comeback, but when I do... you're in for it, Mr. Thrace."

Asher laughed again. "I'll give you a raincheck, but Harper won't, so we better get moving."

They walked together down the hall. Giselle looked around, hoping to see Damien before she went in, but he was nowhere to be found. They'd left on a sour note the day before. That new witch and the sudden way he'd clammed up about her had set her wolf on edge. She didn't like secrets. Too many had been kept from her.

He was supposed to be an open book. Her boyfriend.

After sleeping on it, though, and now that caffeine was jumpstarting her brain, she felt a little more understanding. The whole doctor-patient thing that witches had meant there would be many things he had to keep to himself, and she'd just have to get used to that, as long as they were a couple. And they were a good couple. There was no need to mess with what they had. Damien was one of the few guys in her life who truly understood the whole supernatural thing, and she couldn't fault him for having his own supernatural issues too.

Sadly, that conversation would have to wait until later. As she and Asher walked into Harper's class, she could already see he was in a foul mood. Perhaps he needed a triple shot of espresso too. Maybe that was how she could get on his good side? Giselle made a mental note to grab him a coffee bribe the next morning.

"Richards and Thrace, are you two planning to be partners again this term?" Harper asked, looking down his nose at them with the most evil of smiles.

It didn't take much for Giselle's wolf to rise to the surface. She practically vibrated where she stood, trying to hold back. Asher took her hand. His gesture, surprisingly, soothed her near savageness this morning.

"If that's not a problem, sir," Asher replied.

"You may partner with whomever you wish, but the quality of work had better be up to snuff. This is advanced chemistry, and I will have no messing around." Harper set his gaze back on his desk as if looking at them was no longer worth his time, his warning sufficient to have made his point.

"Of course, sir," Asher said, as calmly as ever.

He was used to taking orders, Giselle assured herself. Mr. Thrace was no softie, and Asher and his brothers no doubt had been housebroken at gunpoint. That thought brought out a giggle and sent her wolf back to sleep. She ducked her head to hide her expression at the inside joke, and slid into her seat at the lab table. "See. I told you he hated me," Giselle whispered to Asher.

Asher shook his head. "Because he warned us to be on our best behavior?"

"Read between the lines."

Asher set his notebook down and pulled out a pen. "You're paranoid."

"Whatever. Downplay it." Giselle got her pen and notebook ready and faced the front of the class, waiting for Mr. Harper to begin a lecture that would no doubt negate the effects of the caffeine she'd just drank.

Written across the board in bold letters was the word *caffeine.*

Giselle nearly burst into laughter.

"Do we find something funny, Miss Richards?" Mr. Harper, sharp as always, zeroed right in on her. And Giselle hadn't really made a spectacle of her laughter either; at least, she didn't think so.

"I think we could all use a little caffeine this morning," Giselle said, trying to sound as if she were not being scolded by her teacher.

"Yes. Well. I thought for the start of term we'd pick an experiment that touched on all of your little lives."

Could that man sound more condescending?

"Show of hands, please. How many of you consumed a caffeinated beverage this morning?"

The entire class raised their hands.

"Just as I thought. In my day, I'd have seen no one with their hand lifted, but that's just a sign of the times. We're going to explore the effects of caffeine on the central nervous system and find the amounts of caffeine present in your favorite beverages of choice, as well as look at alternatives to coffee for the same buzz you get out of caffeine. This will be the focus of the next couple of weeks."

"At least the subject matter is good," Asher whispered to Giselle.

"Only if I can volunteer to drink each and every beverage he comes up with," Giselle responded with a laugh.

"Miss Richards, care to share with the class what you and Mr. Thrace are discussing?"

"Yes, sir. I was saying to Ash that I'd volunteer to drink any of the aforementioned beverages."

Mr. Harper's face contorted with an evil smile. "I'm pleased to hear that, Miss Richards. When we get to tribal herbs and remedies for malaise, you'll be the first I call on for samples."

Shit!

Giselle feigned a smile as she slowly let her head slip to the desk.

She didn't see his face, but she could hear Asher laughing next to her.

This year was already off to a great start.

4

As school days went, her first hadn't been that bad; but still, as soon as the monotony of the day was over, all Giselle could think about was shedding her skin and letting her fur fly free in the breeze. She knew better than to go alone. It was Martina and Gavin's strictest rule, but the call of the night coaxed her wolf from the den of her mind, and would not let go without allowing her to surface. Rules be damned – she knew the open desert behind their neighborhood like the back of her hand, and after months of running with her new pack, she was secure in the fact that no harm would come to her.

A quick run under the moonlight would soothe her wolf, and if she didn't, there would be no sleep tonight. And there was no way she was returning to Harper's class without a good night of sleep. He was already out to get her.

She could have asked Di or Taylor to go with her – that would have been the smart and responsible thing to do – but bringing them along negated her desire to run free. They'd want to stay as a pack and run the same patterns Gavin and Martina took them. She'd get plenty of that next week, when the family ran as a pack under the full moon. Besides, no one would miss her if she snuck out and was back before the lights had been turned off.

Giselle slipped out the back door and headed for the gate. A cloudless sky greeted her, yet even with darkness all around, hardly a twinkle lit the night sky. City life stole some of the heaven's beauty. This wasn't the first time she missed her old home up north. There, life was less noisy, less crowded. Nothing like living in a big city with all the neon and colors that Vegas was famous for. Too much light pollution and a thin layer of smog blotted out the natural beauty of the stars above, and only the brightest ones shone through. Nothing like what she'd seen growing up. Giselle could recall nights where the starlight was enough to brighten her way and let her see the tracks of animals who'd walked through the forest before her. The north had been woodsy, with an earthy feel to it that suited her wolf well. The desert couldn't compare at all: dry and dusty, with hardly a tree in sight. The only benefit here was the vast open space to run. That too came with its problems, though, leaving no place to hide or take shelter if need be. But living up north, she'd had farther to sneak away if she wanted a run. The forest had not been as accessible to her when she lived there. Sneaking out to run had often been problematic, leading to her discovery as a wolf by her human foster parents.

Martina, on the other hand, crafty wolf as she was, had been judicious when she chose this neighborhood, the last development allowed to be built so close to the Sheep mountain range. There would always be open desert for her pack to use.

And smog or no smog, freedom to run was as necessary as air to a wolf.

Giselle pulled the gate shut, ready to strip down and welcome her wolf, but stopped short when an earthy scent caught her attention. Not the musky aroma that accompanied one her own kind; this was perfume, synthetic in nature, something blended to smell natural but that had hints of chemical laced within its aroma. Almost as if someone wanted to smell like a wolf to mask their true scent. Curiosity got the better of her and overcame her wolf's need to run free. She had to know the source of the scent. Her wolf would have to wait.

Giselle allowed her nose to point her in the right direction. If the smell belonged to someone, she'd better find it. The last thing she wanted was to be seen by a neighbor out dumping their trash or taking a late night walk themselves.

The scent floated on the breeze as if it were being directed at her. She picked up traces of it on the gate, and it lingered there as if whomever it belonged to had stood right on that very spot, waiting. She followed its trail, walking slowly, taking her time to find the strongest notes, and allowed the aroma to lead her toward the edge of the service alleyway. She was too busy concentrating and sniffing at the air to notice she'd been spotted.

The sound of someone clearing their throat stopped Giselle dead in her tracks. A woman stood before her staring her down as an Alpha might. But this was no Alpha. She wasn't even a wolf, though her smell was pretty convincing.

Scrambling to give sound to words that caught in her throat, Giselle was rendered speechless by the realization the woman standing in front of her was the same redhead she'd seen the day before at Sammy's.

They eyed each other silently, neither one offering up a word to start the conversation.

In the quiet between them, Giselle studied the scent. Definitely a perfume: natural oils of patchouli had been mixed with clary sage and just a hint of citronella. It worked well to mask the other synthetic smells of deodorant and floral soap that still clung to her body, but not well enough to trick Giselle's nose. This woman was no wolf. She was definitely a witch, though. The pendant she wore was enough to give that away, and the Bohemian style clothing with flowing skirts and odd colorful patterns screamed "earth mother."

The woman closed the distance between them after the silence had long since gone stale. "You do recognize me, don't you?" There was an oddly hopeful edge in the woman's voice that caught Giselle off guard.

Should she recognize her? Sure, they both were redheads. But how many other ginger women in the world were there? That meant nothing. And if she was being truly honest with herself, all the faces of all the foster families that had taken her in and subsequently sent her back into the system had long since blurred together into one wretched image in her mind. If this woman had been a part of the foster system, she was barking up the wrong tree if she thought Giselle would welcome her back into her life with open arms.

"Sorry. No." Giselle crossed her arms in front of her and stood firmly in place.

"Oh, but how could you?" A tear trickled from the corner of the woman's eye. "I just thought... You were such a tiny thing the last time I held you in my arms."

Giselle scoffed silently, remembering all the broken promises and false hope that came with each new family that took her in. "Lots of people held me in their arms... and dropped me just as quickly."

Her words seemed to cut straight to the woman's heart. More waterworks had her wiping her cheeks with the billowy sleeve of her shirt. "I know. I wish I could have given you a different life. You were meant for so much better things. But...I... sorry." She sniffled, taking a few stuttered breaths, and then cleared her throat. "Giselle, I am so very sorry."

"I never told you my name." The woman's tears had tugged at Giselle's heart, but at the mention of her name, she was back on point. How much did this woman know of who she was? And why?

"I didn't mean to come off so forward. I have just been searching for you for so long." The woman reached a hand out as if to welcome her in for a hug, but Giselle took one step backwards, out of her reach.

Giselle opened her mouth to speak, but the words refused to come. The woman had all but admitted to being her mother. She had certainly made a show of emotions. But sad as they were, her sobs failed to stir the same feelings within Giselle. Numbness and confusion had Giselle's feelings locked tighter than a bank vault. If she was her mother... But that wasn't possible. She was no wolf.

That one fact kept her emotions firmly in check. Giselle had given her heart away to too many would-be parents. She'd not let it be broken again on more false hope. Without proof, she could not allow herself to feel anything for this woman, convincing tears or not.

"I shouldn't be here." The woman wiped her face clean with a cloth she'd pulled from her purse. "I really never meant to interfere, but when I finally found out about your adoption, I just had to see... to know you were all right." She stepped in and brushed a stray strand of hair from Giselle's cheek. "Just look at the beautiful woman you've turned into."

Shock had her riveted in place for the moment, but as soon as it wore off, anger set in and she snatched the offending woman's hand as it moved again to touch her hair. "Stop."

The woman's eyes lit with something that bordered on excitement. "And a true Alpha too. I couldn't be prouder."

She'd gone from a sobbing mess to pure delight in the blink of an eye – another red flag that had Giselle's wolf clawing up from within to protect her softer human side from the pain of heartbreak. The wolf gave a strength to Giselle's tone it had not had before. "Look, lady. I don't know what game you're playing."

Excitement faded from the woman's eyes. Her jaw tightened, and she lowered her head slightly as she took a step away. She must have caught the wolf in Giselle's eye. That never failed to send any human backing away.

"I'm so sorry. I shouldn't be intruding. You have a life now. A good one, from the looks of it. I just had to see you once. I promise, I will never darken your door again." The woman looked at the edge of tears and utterly defeated.

Giselle took a long breath to calm herself. Part of her, a very small part, wondered if this woman were speaking the truth. She knew nothing of her past or why she'd ended up in the system. "Just... give me a minute... to process this." She stepped back, giving herself space between them.

Giselle stared down the woman, trying to force herself to recognize something, anything, about her that might make her story true. Even her wolf was hesitant, but the emotion in that woman's eyes tugged at her heart.

"I'm not saying I believe you, but if you think you're connected to me in any way, then explain how this all happened to me."

The woman stiffed and wiped her eyes. "I could say I'm sorry one hundred times, and it wouldn't be enough. I can't even imagine the struggle you must have faced as a wolf among humans." She reached out again as if to take Giselle's hand but pulled back at the last moment.

"How?" Giselle's wolf was back on guard, adding determination and strength to her voice.

"Yours was not a normal birth." The woman's hand moved to her belly, and her head hung in shame. "I could not carry a child to term, and after many unsuccessful attempts we – your father and I – sought the help of a surrogate."

The hairs on the back of Giselle's neck began to prickle. Could this be true? Did she dare allow the fantasy to be real? "How is that possible? You're a witch. I'm a wolf."

"Your father was a wolf, dear. I'm sure you know that supernatural beings occasionally co-mingle. I've seen you with a witch too."

"Spying on me is not helping your case at all." Giselle's tone carried a warning growl.

The woman held her hands up in surrender. "Add it to the list of things I should apologize for. I'm just trying to explain."

Giselle needed to hear more, but worried that she was opening herself to pain again. Her wolf whined within, telling her to stop this madness, but still she opened her mouth and said, "Continue, then."

"As you've probably guessed, the co-mingling was thought to be part of the problem with why I could not carry full term. So our surrogate was a wolf: a beta from your father's pack. Someone we thought we could trust. Nine months we watched and waited. I performed cleansing rituals and fed her strengthening herbs every day of her pregnancy. Everything was perfect. And then she..." Another fresh batch of tears streamed down her cheeks. The woman sniffled and took a breath before continuing. "She disappeared. And try as I might, I could not find you after that."

Giselle had to take a moment to process what she'd just heard. She looked again into the crying woman's eyes for a sign of familiarity, but came up blank. She was saying all the right words, but something still felt off. "She gave no indication as to why she'd left?" Giselle asked with true curiosity. Perhaps there was a clue or something that could fill in the missing piece.

"No!" The woman shook he head and flailed her handkerchief in the air. "We were perfectly happy.

No reason at all. No clue. No nothing. But most of all, no you!"

People didn't just run off like that. There was always a reason. Before Giselle had even made her first full change, she had already seen signs of her foster parents' displeasure. The axe would have fallen for her whether or not she had sprouted a fur coat, and the same with this so-called surrogate. There had to have been some clue in advance. If this story was true. "And what of my father?" Giselle asked, prying further.

"He passed a few years ago. You know how dominance wars can be...." She lowered her head. "I tried to return to my coven, but they rejected me for improper use of magic. I could deal with the loss of my coven, but you... I never lost hope of finding you."

Giselle crossed her arms, scrutinizing every move, each subtle hint of body language. Wolves communicate best through movement, and even when in human form, those little clues of movement revealed more about what was going on with a person than words ever could. This woman gave every indication of true sorrow, down to the trembling fingers and eyes averted to hide the flow of tears. Giselle wanted so much to believe her, but still, she needed more facts. There were too many holes in the story that needed filling. "And how exactly did you manage to locate me?"

"Strange adoptions are not a well-kept secret. I followed several paper trails trying to locate unusual children that matched your expected birth date. And then a few months ago, I found you'd been adopted into a known pack of wolves. Deep down in my soul, I felt it had to be you. Just look at you. So strong. So beautiful. Everything a mother could ever want in her child."

Giselle's wolf took over her voice before she could allow emotions to pull her in. "I'm not your child." If she had been, then why hadn't this woman gone through hell and back to find her?

"No." The woman recoiled as if Giselle might strike at her. "As much as I wish it were true, I failed you. I don't deserve the honor of being called your mother. But not a day goes by that I don't wish I had caught that wretched woman before she took off with you."

"She couldn't have gone far if I ended up in the system. Why didn't she try to raise me? Why run off with a baby and then dump it?" Giselle hadn't meant to speak the words out loud, but the questions demanded answers.

"She knew we'd track her. I wish I could tell you her actions made any sense, but she was found." The woman lifted her head, and the hint of a smile flashed across her face. "She was dealt with. She dropped you at the nearest firehouse after you were born and kept running. That much we got out of her. But by the time we were able to track down the firehouse, your records were sealed. We'd lost you all over again."

Why would a woman run away with someone else's child only to abandon it? That was the most alarming question, and one this woman had avoided answering twice now – a fact that helped Giselle rein in the desire to accept this lady at her word and welcome the mother she'd never had. Reason kept her on point and aloof. "You spin a very interesting tale—" she started to say, but the woman interrupted.

"I don't expect you to trust me. In fact, it's a credit to your nature as an Alpha that you do not. But if you have even the slightest hint in your mind that I am telling you the truth, then maybe we can meet again. After you've taken some time to digest all I've said."

That was the first thing Giselle and the woman could agree on: time was needed to dissect the story and see if it had any grains of real truth to it. "I'll consider it. In broad daylight. Spying on me in the dead of night is not exactly endearing."

"Of course." The woman looked overjoyed at her agreement and started rummaging through her purse as if the contents were of the upmost importance. "Please. Take my card. Call me if you want to talk." The woman handed her a small square with only her name written on one side: Cassandra Atley. She flipped it over and scrawled across the back in loopy script a phone number. "I'll be waiting for you."

And before Giselle could formulate a response, Cassandra turned and walked away, leaving her with a head swarming with questions.

Could she really have been the mother Giselle had dreamed of all her life? The thought took hold of her and would not let go. All those years wondering. Nights spent crying into her pillow feeling abandoned and unwanted. This Cassandra certainly looked the part. But if it were true, what would it all mean? She'd only just settled into a new family.

5

Lost between the reality she knew and the new fantasy of having a blood relative, a mother, had Giselle's head spinning so fast that even her wolf refused to surface. She abandoned all plans of taking her midnight run and snuck back into the house, hoping to meet with silence to allow herself time to process everything. Instead she found Taylor sitting on her bunk with her face glued to her computer screen.

"Well, that was quick," Taylor said, as Giselle walked back into the bedroom. She closed the lid of her laptop and looked up with more curiosity than should have been afforded a quick sneak out to run.

"I didn't think anyone would notice I had left." Giselle slumped down on her bed.

"You're not as sneaky as you think, you know." Taylor laughed. "You could have just asked. I could have used a run myself."

"Well, you both seemed busy. Where's Di?" Giselle asked.

"Bath. Melting away the stress of the day and working on her exfoliating regime." Taylor stood and placed her laptop on the desk.

A bath and some quiet time sounded pretty good to Giselle. "I call dibs next."

Taylor walked over and sat next to Giselle on the bed. "You've been off lately. And I know it's not the new school year. What's up?"

Taylor's show of sisterly solidarity made her smile inwardly, but she couldn't allow it to show on her face. Too much confusion had her emotions all over the place, and until she could make sense of it all, she wouldn't be ready to share with anyone, even her well-meaning sister. "I'm fine. You haven't known me long enough. New school years always give me this kind of stress."

"If you say so." Taylor shrugged, but the roll of her eyes said she wasn't buying Giselle's excuse.

Giselle stood and walked across the room, pretending to be interested in picking out an outfit from the closet. That always worked to distract her sisters. "I do. And I'll be even better after I settle what to wear tomorrow."

Taylor perked up as expected and joined her at the closet, instantly locating a pair of skinny jeans for Giselle to wear. "Oh, I forgot to tell you – Damien called while you were out."

"Why didn't he text me?" Giselle responded.

"He talked to Di. Said something about witchy business and to keep the pack together." She spoke nonchalantly, but there was a hint of unease there just below the surface. "Oh, and wear that faux leather shrug with the lavender tank top. It'll look hot." She pulled the top off the hanger and let it fall into Giselle's outstretched hands.

Giselle couldn't care less about the clothes, especially seeing how Taylor had deliberately used them to change the subject. "So, Damien felt the need to tell that to Di rather than me? What the hell is that about?"

"I thought that was funny too." Taylor shrugged, but her eyes said it clearly that she wanted to drop the subject. "But you know... Don't kill the messenger."

"I'm supposed to be his girlfriend. He could have talked to me directly. He has my cell number." Giselle hadn't meant to direct her annoyance at Taylor and instantly felt bad for her outburst. Taylor had done nothing more than relay a message. It was Damien she wanted to snap at. Lowering her head in shame, Giselle offered a quiet, "Sorry," and set down the clothes she'd been holding. "I like purple. It's a pretty color. Thanks for picking it out."

Taylor shook her head and sighed. "Look. Talk to Di when she gets out of the bath. I'm sure there's nothing bad is going on, and there's a perfectly good explanation for why Damien decided to talk to her first."

"It's probably because of that new witch in town." No question about it. That *had* to be the reason.

Taylor walked back to her bunk and stretched out. "The one that got your hackles up?"

"Yeah. You saw her try and stare me down. She's...." Giselle was this close to revealing her encounter with the woman but held back at the last moment. She couldn't put a finger on what it was about that woman, but she couldn't condemn her just yet. Nor could she trust her. She needed to find out more, to see if there were any truth to the story she'd told about her birth and adoption. "She's up to something. That's for sure. But what?"

"You think she's a bad witch?" Taylor asked.

"I'll bet Damien knows. That's why he told Di to keep us together. He wants to make sure I don't do anything stupid."

"Why would you?" Taylor turned a curious eye on Giselle.

"Because..." She wondered if she should clue her sister in on what had happened. If she did, would Taylor be on her side, or take Damien's view and try to keep her out of it?

"Because?" Taylor asked, looking even more determined to get an answer from Giselle.

"You know me." Giselle tried to play it off with a shrug and a giggle. "Can't leave a good mystery alone."

"True enough." Taylor appeared to have accepted her at her word. She laid her head back on the pillow and stared up at her posters on the underside of Di's bunk.

Thank goodness for that. Giselle knew her sisters meant well, but when she herself didn't quite know what to think, she wasn't fully ready to lay the burden of this new information in their laps. Especially when her boyfriend had already shown his cards. No matter what she said, he was already trying to keep her away from Cassandra. But that wasn't what bothered her most. The *why* behind it was far more intriguing. What had this woman done to earn herself such a black mark as to be shunned by witches even as far south as Vegas? That in itself was reason enough for her to doubt the story she'd been told. Still, though, part of her wanted to believe.

Di walked in, her hair wrapped in a towel and another around her body. "Back already, Giselle?" She cast a sidelong glance at her sister as she passed on her way to the closet.

"Yeah. I hear Damien has a crush on you? I found out about your secret phone call." Giselle feigned anger.

Di pulled on a pair of comic book printed pants and a blue cami and then tossed her towel straight at Giselle. "He does not. And what secret phone call? Taylor was standing right there. He said his cousin is in town and she's got the family all busy with rituals and whatnot, so I should keep you occupied so you don't get all jealous... like you clearly are."

Damn, he was a bad liar, and Di too. What the hell?

"Well, if that's all, then I guess... I call dibs on the bathroom." Giselle smiled sweetly and scooped up the towel at her feet.

"That's it? You get all possessive and accusing me of stealing your man, and then just drop it?" Di asked.

"You know I'm just playing with you. I know you're not stealing Damien from me."

"Well, of course not... but I could if I wanted to," Di smirked.

"Right. Go ahead." Giselle tossed the towel back across the room at her sister.

Di snatched the towel in mid-air and snapped it like a whip. "Is that a challenge?"

"Don't be bitchy. But don't lie to me either. Damien didn't feed you a line of crap to tell me. So don't think I'll just take what you said at face value."

Di rolled her eyes. "Fine. Whatever. He said to keep you busy so you'd stop looking into the new witch in town. His coven is dealing with it."

"Was that so hard?" Giselle asked.

"Why did you lie to her?" Taylor asked.

Di huffed. "You have that boy wrapped around your finger, and it's breaking him. Witch business is not our business. Him prying into things he shouldn't and then relaying them to you is causing trouble at home. He was my friend first. I don't like seeing him stressed out."

Finally some honesty. Giselle put her hands to her hips and stared at Di, daring her silently to snap the towel again. "Then say that. Be honest. Don't be a bitch."

"Why don't you tone down the attitude yourself, sister?" Di said, tossing the towel down to the ground at her feet.

"I will when people stop treating me like some precious little child who can't handle herself."

"You are a child. We all are. Enjoy it while it lasts," Di said.

"My childhood was nothing like yours. I was forced to grow up years ago. Excuse me for demanding to be given a bit of respect." Giselle said.

"No one is saying you're not worthy of respect. But Di has a point." Taylor was on her feet, standing between Di and Giselle. "You're still new to our way of life. Maybe try being less demanding and more trusting that we all have each other's back."

"Then maybe my sisters shouldn't lie to me," Giselle said.

"It goes both ways. Next time you try to sneak out, remember that," Di said. "You could have trusted us with that knowledge, at least.

"Fine." Giselle flounced on her bunk, ending the conversation but not the thoughts running through her mind. Too many questions. Too many inconsistencies. And worse, she'd alienated her sisters, the ones she was supposed to rely on. Maybe she should tell them what was bothering her.

6

Giselle waited outside of Damien's locker, intent on ripping him a new one. It was one thing for her to have secrets from her sisters. He was supposed to be different. He was her boyfriend and her liaison to the witches, and the bastard had gone behind her back.

When she finally spotted him coming around the corner, she took off, all predator ready for the kill, witnesses be damned. Giselle rushed through the hallway intent on catching him, but ran straight into him when he stopped dead in his tracks, and they tumbled together to the floor.

Laughter and chatter from students in the hall brought her back to reality, and embarrassment colored her cheeks. She stood and helped Damien to his feet before retrieving her fallen books.

"I should have expected that, I guess." Damien didn't even sound mad. And that confirmed it for Giselle that he'd been in the wrong.

"Di. You called Di before talking to me," Giselle said, a little louder than she'd intended. The entire school was already talking about her. Now they'd get a front row seat to her and Damien's fight. No doubt the gossip mill was already churning out stories about their relationship troubles, though they could never fathom the true strangeness of their partnership.

"Di and I go way back. I knew she'd understand the rules." Damien made no attempt to sound apologetic, and that further infuriated Giselle.

"And I am somehow incapable of understanding?" Giselle snarled at him.

Damien backed away a step, holding his hand out in surrender. "You've been really on edge these last couple weeks. I don't know if it's the moon or..."

"Don't you dare finish that sentence!" If looks could kill, Damien would have been dead on the ground. Why did guys always have to blame women's issues?

"Whoa, whoa, whoa." Damien took another step back. "You know what I mean. When the moon rises, you all become a bit more animal." His voice warbled. She'd never seen him so nervous. But that wasn't going to get him off that easy.

"And Di is still okay to talk to, over me? Did you forget she's like me?"

"Look, I'm clearly not going to win this argument. Can I just apologize now, and we can move on to making up? That's the best part anyway." Always the jokester. Giselle had to admit his deflection and easygoing manner were disarming, but she wasn't going to back down so easily. She needed more than an apology. She wanted answers.

"I'll let you buy me a burger for lunch, but only if you tell me what you know."

"And how do you know I know anything?" Damien asked.

"Really?" She eyed him, more wolf than woman at that point, just daring him to continue to annoy her with his evasiveness.

"Yes. Fine. I'll talk... and buy you a burger. If for no other reason than to take myself off the menu."

"I don't know why you'd hide things from me in the first place." Giselle allowed him to lead her down the hallways toward the cafeteria.

"I don't hide things on purpose. You know how our kind operate: we have rules and things... you might not always want to follow them, but some of us have to." Damien opened the door to the cafeteria, and they lined up at an order window. "You might not believe me, but I want to see you happy. And stressing out over this lady is not going to make that happen."

Giselle allowed him to drone on as they waited for the line to move, not sure what she wanted to say to him. The smell of the food, if it could be called that, was distracting enough to her starving wolf. She needed meat; lots of it. Damien had one thing right: as the moon grew closer to being full, she was more animal, and hers want agitated and hungry at the moment.

When their turn came, Damien ordered two burgers for Giselle and a basket of onion rings for himself, and then they walked to the table.

"You're not talking," Damien said.

Giselle had spent all that time debating on whether or not she should tell him about the witch. He had already said she should stay away. But in the interest in full disclosure, both of them needed to come clean. If he would, so would she.

"How about this... I tell you what I know about this witch, and you do the same. I think you'll be surprised how much information I got on her without your help."

"Fair enough. I can confirm what I know to be true. How's that?"

"Not exactly full disclosure then, is it?"

"You know I have to keep some things on the down low."

"Whatever." Damn witches and their secrets! She took a bite of her burger and then said, "The witch says she's my mom."

Damien spit his drink across the table. "Your what?"

Giselle laughed at the shocked expression on Damien's face, and managed to save his onion rings from being drowned in soda as he knocked it over trying to grab a napkin. "Yeah, that's what I thought."

"Can't be. She's a witch. And not a nice one, either. I'm not sure how much is rumor and how much is fact, but supposedly she comes from a coven that was excommunicated about ten years ago."

"Seriously? Excommunicated?" There wasn't an eye-roll big enough to properly convey her sarcasm. "Are you like Rome or something? Are we in the 1400's?"

Damien's expression soured. He wiped up as much of the spilled soda he could, creating a mountain of wet napkins on the table. "Look. Her coven were assholes. No good witch or coven was to associate with them any longer. Is that more twentieth century for you?"

Giselle pushed Damien's basket of onion rings back in front of him and winked. "You're still out of date, dude."

"Oh, you're in rare form today, aren't you?" He fake laughed and quickly snatched up a greasy ring, shoving it into his mouth.

"Sorry, yeah. It's just, she got me all... I don't know."

"She gave you the feels, and now you're getting girly about it, huh?"

"Seriously... turn down the asshole. Okay?"

"I'm just playing. What did she tell you?"

"Like I'm going to tell you now, Captain Asshole."

Damien reached a hand out to grab Giselle's food. "I bought you a burger, remember? Legally binding contract to spill the beans."

Giselle smacked his hand away. "Verbal contract isn't worth anything."

"Not to a witch...." Damien waggled one of his eyebrows at her and she couldn't help but laugh at his cocky attitude. "You word is your oath to us."

Damn witchy mumbo-jumbo. "Whatever. Fine. She didn't say much. Just that she was my mom and lost me as a baby because of..." She hesitated, trying to come up with a convincing half-truth, hoping he'd fill in the blanks with the real information. "Wolf-witch politics. I dunno. It's all weird."

"I get it. She threw out a plausible story. You're confused. But trust me. She's not your mom. Word from my coven is, that lady is no good, and will be asked to leave very soon. Let it slide, and in a week or so, this will all just be a memory."

So much for getting information out of him. Giselle softened her approach, smiling as she unwrapped her burger. "But... what if..."

Damien met her eyes with determination befitting one of her own kind. "She. Can't. Be."

His sudden flip from casual had her interest more than piqued. Why get so touchy, when she'd hardly said anything about the woman?

"Why not? Her story has some" – she couldn't say the word *sense* because even to her, it all sounded a little strange, but she had nothing else to put into that sentence – "good points."

Damien sighed. "The whole wolves and witches thing has never worked... *in that way*."

"That's what she said, so she had a surrogate."

"Convenient." Damien stuffed another onion ring into his mouth.

"It's not unheard of."

"For humans. Regular. Normal. Humans."

"So, what? Supernaturals don't have infertility issues?"

Damien nearly choked on his food. "Look. I'm totally not comfy with the whole baby making discussion. I still have nightmares about the talk my mom tried to give me, and that was years ago. Check with Martina. She'll tell you how it works. And yes... she had issues too, remember?"

"Well, just remember that squeamishness the next time you forget a condom..."

Damien cringed and quickly hid his face in his hands. "That's a low blow."

"You left yourself wide open for that one. You had to know I'd take the opportunity."

"Touché, wolfy..."

"Seriously, though. I can't help but think that there's some truth to her story. And even if it isn't true, why is she here now? Why did she present herself to me?"

"Good questions. Wish I knew." Damien sighed impatiently. "All Mom said was, she's bad news, and it's being handled by the coven. That's why I asked Di to keep you occupied. Let us deal with her in our own way before things get weird."

"You could have just told me that. You know, honesty, trust..."

"I'm sorry. Really. Bad boyfriend... bad!" He smacked himself in the cheek. "Never do that again. See. I've learned my lesson. Can we be friends again?"

Giselle tried to hold back her laughter and ended up snorting loudly enough for kids the next table over to take notice. Though still annoyed with his actions, Giselle couldn't help but appreciate the way he always made her laugh. It helped to soften her attitude enough for her to accept his apology... for now. "Fine. But next time you pull something stupid like that, I get to smack you."

The lunch bell rang before Giselle could finish her burger. She shoveled it into her mouth, earning a grimace from Damien before he stood to walk away.

"Can I catch a ride home with you and the girls later?" Damien called after her.

"Check with Di. I have something I need to do after school." Before he could ask what, she walked away.

7

When the final bell rang, Giselle bolted out of school as fast as she could, hoping to avoid her sisters, Damien, and even Asher. She'd asked Cassandra to meet her at the park down the hill from school, and she didn't want to have to explain herself just yet.

Backpack in hand, she ran down the street with all the speed of a horror movie victim attempting to escape a predator, only slowing down when she saw the long red hair of the witch in the distance; she was sitting alone on a park bench. The scent of her wafted up to Giselle's nose again, the wolf-like aroma that nearly fooled her the first time they met, but this time Giselle picked up the immediate undertones of synthetic additives. She wondered if the perfume were intentional or just one of her witchy quirks. After all, Damien often had a hint of oil under his overwhelming scent of body spray.

After school was prime time at the park. A good time for a public chat, she thought.

Children were playing around her on the equipment, laughing and shrieking as kids do, but it was the peaceful, serene look on Cassandra's face that made her truly take notice. She looked on as if she were one of the proud parents watching their little ones master the monkey bars.

Giselle had always wondered what it would be like to have had a mother to care for her like that. What would life have been like if Mommy had been there to push her on the swing or chase pigeons in the park with her? Would she have grown up to be so stubborn if she'd had help on the monkey bars, instead of always being left to her own devices?

Her foster parents had largely let her figure things out on her own. They'd been busy with their own lives, for the most part. She'd had food, shelter, and clothes, of course. All the necessities had been there; but never the love of a true parent. Even now, watching the mothers of little children hovering around, making sure their little one didn't fall or miss a step as they climbed up to the slide, made her long for memories of her own mother doing the same. But she had no memory of anyone caring enough to do that for her.

There was something else beyond her own sense of lost love; she saw it clear as day on Cassandra's face. She'd never stopped to think of the other side. What if Cassandra had been telling the truth, and she too had been robbed of moments like these?

Some of the other mothers at the park looked distracted. Between catching their little ones on the slide and pushing them in their swings, many of them focused on their phones or chatted amongst themselves. But not Cassandra; she watched each child with rapt adoration.

Oh, the feels. Get a grip, Elle! She gave herself a mental slap. There was still no proof of what Cassandra had said earlier, and if she was to be truly honest with herself, Giselle wasn't sure she wanted there to be. She had a good thing going now with Martina, Gavin, and her new sisters. Why wreck it with a mother who had never been there?

"I don't know why I agreed to this," Giselle said, as she came up behind Cassandra.

"Because you know, deep down in your heart of hearts, that I am right." Cassandra stood and reached out her arms, probably to hug Giselle, but then hesitated and stepped back.

Giselle stood just out of reach. "Let's not go that far."

Cassandra smiled, but the strain behind her expression showed through. "Your skepticism is a good thing. I'm glad you're not blindly accepting of me. It shows how strong of an Alpha you are. Question everything. Get to the bottom of this mystery. It will make our reunion all the sweeter."

"I need to know more. How...Why?" Giselle asked.

"For wolves, family is everything. Witches too. The passing of our lineage on to the next generation. Ensuring traditions, memories, and our blood lives on." She held a hand out, indicating the walking path, and took a step to lead them both on.

Giselle followed along, keeping Cassandra to her left, hugging the edge of the sidewalk. "But you're a witch, and my father... presumably a wolf."

"Of course he was a wolf, dear. You are proof of that."

"Why mix" – Giselle struggled for the right word – "species?"

"Because we wanted a family." Cassandra's expression soured, somewhere between confusion and sadness. "There doesn't need to be any additional reason. We were in love and wanted to start a life together, outside of the packs and the covens and all the tedium that goes with that. We wanted it to be just us... family."

"But that didn't work... you couldn't have a child with him. You needed the pack." She hadn't meant it to sound so harsh, but she'd rather not pussyfoot around the issue.

"Sadly, yes." Cassandra hung her head and took a breath. "And your father took quite a lot of grief for it. An Alpha is supposed to sire the next generation of Alphas. He didn't care. He had brothers who could take the reins as Alpha and do that duty."

Wolf politics. That was a subject that vexed Giselle on a regular basis. Being a loner for so long, she'd been blissfully unaware of the rigidity of pack life. Honor to your pack and doing what *they* wished over your own desires was what was expected; listening to someone just because they were called *Alpha*. Beyond family obligations, pack life was like joining the military for life. Though admittedly, Martina's pack was very easygoing in comparison to the Thrace pack. Thankfully she'd ended up where she did. Wolf or not, she'd have never lasted in Thrace's pack. They'd have found a way to get rid of her for all the trouble she caused. Giselle snorted to herself thinking of it.

"Something funny?" Cassandra asked.

That brought her back on track. She cleared her throat. "No. Nothing. So, the witches' coven. How did they handle it?"

"Witches are so much more forgiving than wolves, dear."

Giselle might have been distracted before, but now she was riveted to the witch. There was something off; something she just couldn't put words to. Cassandra had an air about her of motherly love, but in that last answer, something spoke of veiled anger and resentment. Lies always came with a tell, and Giselle could usually spot one a mile away, but there were too many question marks hanging around and she hadn't known Cassandra long enough to use good judgment. Either way, Giselle was certain of one thing: she needed to keep Cassandra at arm's length until she learned more. Letting emotion or daydreams of the perfect mom get in the way was bound to cause more pain.

Cassandra let out a deep sigh, as if trying to draw attention to herself rather than convey longing.

Giselle gave her a nod and continued her interrogation. "There had to be some kind of expectation, though, around a mixed baby."

"Honestly... a union between species is not a common thing. We knew not what to expect. We only hoped for a happy, healthy baby."

Giselle didn't believe that for a moment. A wolf with witch abilities. That could be quite a powerful blend. If it worked. They had to have considered that as a possibility. But she allowed Cassandra's lie to slip past as they walked further along the path.

Silence stretched between them. Giselle wondered what life might have been like for her had she remained with Cassandra. If she truly was her mother, and had the chance to raise her. Cassandra looked to be a woman of comfort. Well-dressed. Hair and nails all kept trim and tidy. Fingers adorned with pretty rings.

A far cry from the single luggage-worth of belongings Giselle had kept her entire life.

She gave herself another mental slap. She was supposed to be keeping her wits about her, and already she was letting her guard down.

"I still can't say I believe you. But you do present an interesting story."

"It's not a story," Cassandra said sharply.

"It is until it checks out," Giselle answered.

"But don't you feel it? We're so alike, you and I. We even look the same."

"Everyone has a doppelganger."

"You are such an Alpha." Cassandra sniffled and wiped at her nose. "I should be proud. Go, then. Go seek the answers you are looking for. I will be here, and you obviously know my phone number."

"How long will you be here? Aren't you supposed to check in with the local coven?"

Cassandra's eyes darkened. Her lip twitched at the corner like someone hiding behind gritted teeth pretending to be okay. "Of course. Well, you know how that goes. You have that witch friend."

"I do. And he tells me everything that goes on in the coven."

"Certainly not everything." Cassandra was quickly developing a nervous tic, grabbing at her arm as if it were itching. "Remember, dear. Just like wolf politics, witches too have their rules and regulations. Nothing is ever simple with us."

Her whole body was giving off panic signals, which wasn't helping her case at all with Giselle. Clearly Cassandra had issues with the local coven. And from what Damien said, the feeling was more than mutual. That helped Giselle harden her heart in the face of this woman who looked like she very well could be the long lost mother Giselle had always dreamed of.

"You should take care of whatever witchy business you need to, then. I'll be in touch." Giselle gave a slight nod and held her hand out to shake.

Cassandra looked as if she'd been offered the world, eagerly taking hold of Giselle's hand and giving it a loving squeeze. "Please do call on me again. Please."

Giselle had to fight to pull her hand from Cassandra's grip, and as she walked away, her heart and mind warred with each other.

8

The walk home had given her even more worry. Between entertaining thoughts of a real relationship with her mom and the question marks hanging above the witch's head, she didn't know what to think anymore. But then, she had a mom now. Not a witch popping up out of the blue when she least needed it, but a good, caring mother in Martina.

Everything Giselle could have ever hoped for, Martina had taken her in and treated her like family from the moment she'd laid eyes on Giselle. With Martina, there was no question that she loved and accepted Giselle as she was, even if she was more than a bit of a troublemaker.

How much would it break Martina's heart to hear she might belong to someone else? Further to that, if Cassandra did have a claim, would Giselle have to leave the pack? She'd only just settled into life as a real wolf with a real family.

She'd walked nearly half an hour before reaching home, and that hadn't been long enough to settle her mind down. As she approached the driveway, a new car caught her attention. Sleek, black, and sporty, it was definitely not Martina's or

Gavin's. That meant company. A distraction might be just what she needed to give herself more time to think. Giselle cracked open the door slowly, intending to sneak up to her room unnoticed, but Martina was there, ambushing her as she stepped one toe into the busy, packed house.

"Oh, good. You're home. Wash up. We have company." Kitchen knife in hand, Martina blew past her, heading toward the kitchen to chop vegetables.

Before she could respond, Giselle picked up the cloying scent of wet earth. This was the real deal, not a fabricated perfume like Cassandra wore. There were more wolves than normal in her home. Through the back sliding glass door she could see the backs of what looked like four new people as well as Gavin, all congregating around the grill. "Were we expecting someone?" Giselle asked.

"This is Vegas, dear; unexpected company is normal." Martina's tone said otherwise, but Giselle knew better than to press the point with her now. The girls were already in the house. She picked up on their scent, a mix of wolf and Candy Kisses perfume wafting through the air.

"Tay and Di upstairs?" she asked.

"Yes, and you can tell them to get down here and help with dinner too."

"Okay. Will do." Giselle rushed up the stairs and found Taylor and Di mid-fashion show in their bedroom. "Explain," she said, interrupting the preening session.

"Did you see them?" Taylor turned away from staring at herself in the vanity mirror mid-mascara and met Giselle's eyes.

"No, but I could smell them coming through the door. How many are here?" Unexpected visitors weren't necessarily a good thing in Giselle's mind. Still new to all this pack business, she felt a little reassurance seeing her sisters so focused on looking their best. At least that meant there was no immediate danger.

"Like a whole pack," Taylor responded eagerly. "Four at least. And none of them girls."

Di stepped out of the closet wearing a floral print babydoll dress and white espadrilles. "Yeah, and there are two hot brothers I'd like to get to know a little better."

"Why have they come?" Giselle asked.

"Who knows? Pack politics. Arranged marriages. Could be anything," Taylor said, a little more excitedly than she probably should have been at the thought of marriage. They were still in high school, for god's sake. Who got excited over being tied down like that?

"Is that seriously still a thing?" Giselle asked, praying the answer would be no, but given her relative newness to the whole pack dynamic thing, anything was possible.

"Yeah. Very much so," Di answered, putting the finishing touches on her makeup and ending with a smooch to herself in the mirror.

"Doesn't really matter, the *why* part; they're here now, and Martina is super-stressed with making them feel at home, so we better finish up and go entertain," Taylor said.

"I'm ready." Di stood and gave a little wiggle to her reflection in the closet mirror. "Dressed to impress and entertain.

"Well, Elle isn't, and she looks like she's going to take a lot of work," Tay huffed.

"Wow, thanks!" Giselle grumbled, as she took a quick look in the mirror. Her ponytail was intact, sporting only a few stray hairs. And what was wrong with jeans and a t-shirt, anyway? She didn't need to be runway-ready every day. That was way too much work.

"I didn't mean it like that. You've just come home from a run, or something. Your hair is a little windblown. You need an outfit, some makeup, and maybe a hit or two of perfume."

"Still sounds like you're calling me a slob," Giselle grumbled.

"Shut up and let me dress you. You know I live for this kind of thing," Taylor said.

Di snickered and headed for the door. "Dibs on the cute one."

"Brat! Which one's the cute one?" Taylor asked.

"Don't know, but finders keepers." She stuck her tongue out at Taylor and disappeared through the door.

"Really... you two." Giselle laughed.

"Hey, neither of us have hottie boyfriends."

Giselle caught the air of jealousy in Taylor's tone. She wondered about Asher and what had gone on between them. They had seemed like they could have been the next high school power couple, and they still talked in the halls, but Taylor's mood about boyfriends had cooled quite a bit over the summer.

"Do I dare mention—"

"No. You don't. Now march yourself over here so I can dress you."

Taylor picked out a pair of capri pants and a deep-V button-up sleeveless linen shirt in emerald green for Giselle to wear and topped it off with a long beaded necklace tied mid-way down the V. "Casual, yet sophisticated. The only thing now is a cute messy bun and a pair of dangly earrings, and you'll be set."

It was more than Giselle would have picked out for herself, but she had to admit, the transformation was perfect. Taylor was going to make it big in fashion, there was no doubt about that. The girl had talent. She managed to make the look effortless, though when she saw how long they'd been upstairs playing dress up, she knew she'd be in trouble.

"Just a quick spritz." Taylor perfume-bombed her with something overpoweringly floral, and Giselle found herself nearly choking as she was ushered out of the room.

9

Stepping out into the living space of the house, even from their lofty height at the top of the stairs, Giselle could have cut the tension with a knife. This was no mere social call. Or, if it was, the importance of the people visiting had put everyone on edge, and the sensation was nothing short of creepy.

The conversation below, which should have bordered on boisterous with all the people congregating, was calm and almost cautious.

Giselle looked below before taking her first step down. Four men, just as Taylor had said, were sitting in the living room with Gavin and Di.

Definitely wolves. The scent of wet earth would be enough for humans to pick up, as thick as it was. All dark-haired except for one, the most well-dressed of the bunch, each of them had the natural bulk Giselle was beginning to associate with her kind. Not massive or unhealthy looking, but strong. Just one look at them, even from behind, and she felt they could hold their own in a fight. *Their wolves must look magnificent*, she thought.

The red-haired man, clearly the leader of the group, stood near the fireplace, a drink in hand. He spotted Giselle at the top landing and immediately turned to the man sitting at his right and whispered something.

"Get moving, girl." Taylor ushered Giselle forward.

She should have moved, but her feet refused to budge.

Martina was still banging and clanging away in the kitchen, cursing under her breath, but even upstairs, Giselle could hear her. Everyone had supernatural hearing, but none of the group below dared to even chuckle when she uttered some very loud frustrated curse, though a few cracked smiles at the more colorful words Martina had chosen.

The formality in the way everyone was acting set Giselle's wolf on edge. Two of the newcomers looked to be about Giselle's age, and though they had been the ones to smile when Martina began cursing, they sat almost stone still and cast quick glances at the redhead as if seeking his approval for even that small lapse of stoicism.

"I don't like this," Giselle whispered.

Taylor shoved past her and grabbed hold of Giselle's arm. "We can't wait up here all day. We're already late in introducing ourselves."

They descended into the living room with all eyes zeroing in on them like a spotlight. The scrutinizing gaze of everyone, especially the red-haired man, had Giselle's wolf clawing its way to the surface, ready to face the unspoken challenge.

"These are the last two in your pack?" one of the males, an older man with a head of wavy hair working all the way down to his full beard asked. "Just the girls, then?"

Gavin stood and waved a hand in their direction. "Ours is an unusual pack, of course. But yes, these are the last two of my girls." He smiled proudly and introduced Taylor first and then Giselle.

The red-haired man nodded to each of them, but his eyes lingered on Giselle longer than felt comfortable.

He was the Alpha; Giselle could feel it in her bones as she looked at him.

After the moment was over, he looked back at his group and introduced them. "These are my boys, Ace and Jay, and my second, Richard." He indicated the younger boys and then the man with the full beard who'd spoken first. "I'm David Silverman." His haunting eyes refused to leave Giselle's face, as if her reaction were somehow important.

Giselle smiled politely and nodded, breaking eye contact, against the urging of her own wolf to challenge him. "What's the occasion?" she asked, getting straight to the point, rather than wasting time in mindless chat.

David smiled; amused perhaps, or maybe he too was just being polite. "Regular little Alpha you have on your hands, Gavin." He turned to address her adopted father.

Gavin's lips pursed for a moment as if he were holding back what he wanted to say. He cast a warning glare at Giselle before responding to David. "We're very proud of how strong of will all of our girls are."

"Is it true they're all adopted?" David asked, casting his eyes over the other two girls quickly.

Gavin's body tensed. "Yes. My wife and I have not been able to... well, there's no need to discuss these things in front of the children."

David smiled politely and nodded his head as if to say he understood, but his focus shifted to Giselle again like she was the only thing of real interest in the room.

She almost snarled at him this time as her wolf rose up, feeling threatened by this unknown man giving so much attention to her, silently challenging her. The wolf stared back at her through his eyes. Powerful, strong, and... familiar, in a way. But the unwelcome eye contact was something her wolf could not abide. Driven by instinct, she nearly let her wolf rise up, but held back long enough for the glance to be over with.

Gavin set down his drink on the coffee table. Tense and moving as if each step were calculated, he stood and joined Giselle and Taylor at the base of the stairs. "They'll only be here for a day or so," he whispered, as he took both girls' hands. His grip spoke volumes of his level of stress, and his tone warned of the status these men had.

Not sure if she knew quite how to act around them, Giselle took a breath and tried to send her wolf back down. She squeezed Gavin's hand as a sign of solidarity and allowed him to guide her and Taylor into the living room.

David, still standing at the fireplace, widened his smile to a full toothy grin, and though he was in human form, the sharpness of his teeth further proved his supernatural nature. "What an interesting pack, indeed."

With his eyes glued to her, all alarms were going off in her head. The creeper vibe was strong with this one.

"Would that we had a few strong girls like yours in our pack, Gavin," David continued, with a little wink of his eye.

Gavin squeezed her hand again, and Giselle wasn't sure what unspoken message he was trying to convey, but she couldn't shake the uneasy feeling this guy was giving her.

"David, right? You didn't answer me, before." Giselle realized her tone was bordering on rude, and attempted to soften the last bit. "What brings you here to visit us?"

David's lip curled almost imperceptibly, but Giselle caught the annoyance directed at her rude tone.

The two boys, Ace and Jay, had caught it as well. One brought his hand to his mouth with a small gasp, and the other lowered his head to the ground, as if not wanting to witness the retribution for someone daring to be so rude.

Di gritted her teeth so hard Giselle could pick it up from across the living room.

Yeah, she'd messed up. No backpedaling out of this one. Even Taylor was shaking her head.

Giselle looked to Gavin for guidance, but he dropped his head with a sigh, releasing Giselle's hand at the same time.

She could have apologized for her words, but somehow it didn't feel it would do any good. Giselle feigned an awkward smile and found an open seat on the couch.

David's silence and creeper stare only intensified as she took her seat. He waited until both she and

Taylor had taken their places before responding, "I'm showing my boys the reach of our territory."

Of course she would have to piss off the Grand High Poobah of wolves. The creeper vibe vanished as she realize he'd been sizing her up this whole time and had obviously found her lacking in... every way possible.

"Forgive me for my ignorance." Giselle tried to smooth over her initial roughness. "I'm new and all. Been a foster kid, not a pack animal, my whole life. We have territories?" She finished with a shrug and a chuckle that she hoped would earn her a little forgiveness.

"It's quite all right. All wolves need to know their place." David's gaze locked onto Giselle. The message was clear that she was overstepping her bounds. "Giselle, is it?" He didn't wait for her to answer. "There are pack alphas" – his eyes flashed quickly to Gavin and then back to her – "and then there are Regional Alphas. Can you guess which one I am?"

The pompous attitude gave that one away easily. Giselle repressed a snort, playing it off as a coughing fit, and took a calming breath before asking. "What region do you cover, then?

"Very good." David's condescending tone grated on Giselle's nerves, but she knew better than to rise to the occasion now, especially when she'd already overstepped once this evening, and Gavin looked like he was ready for murder. Giselle smiled innocently and waited for David to continue. "I'm Alpha over the pacific region."

"Like the time zone?" She tried to sound as interested as she could, and hoped the ruse would pass.

Ace, or maybe it was Jay, snorted and covered his hand as if he were trying to play off a cough as Giselle had moments earlier.

David sent him a warning look. "Essentially, yes. Let's go with that for now." He nodded at Giselle. "It's my job to check up on all the packs under me and make sure everything is up to code. No rule breaking. No revealing yourselves to humans... that kind of thing."

"Are we in any trouble?" Taylor asked, genuinely sounding worried.

"No," David replied with a chuckle. Finally someone had taken the attention away from Giselle, and she was so thankful. "This is simply a social visit. Though I have to admit, I have heard some interesting stories about your pack and the Thrace pack recently. Mended fences and all."

"All thanks to Elle," Taylor said proudly. "She brought everyone back together."

"Lovely." David sounded less impressed and turned his attention to Gavin. "And the sister... Christine? Where is she?" he asked.

Gavin cleared his throat before speaking. "She's celebrating her honeymoon. Catalina Island Cruise, I believe."

"Ah. Poor timing. I'd have love to have seen her, after all she's been through."

Martina called for everyone to join her in the dining room, and Giselle had never been happier for the distraction. She snatched Taylor's hand, preventing her from walking off. "I don't like him." Every one of her senses screamed that this David guy was up to something. But what?

"Shhh. Don't you dare say that out loud. You heard him. He's the main wolf!"

"He may be, but he's not here to parade his boys around. He's got an ulterior motive. I just know it."

"Keep it to yourself while he's here, then. Play nice," Taylor urged.

"I'll try." Giselle stood put on her best smile and allowed Taylor to drag her into the dining room.

10

Dinner had been the most awkward affair she'd ever encountered. Gavin was so wound up he chewed his cheek more than his steak, and Martina nearly spilled the pitcher of water on David when she went to offer him a drink. Conversation, if anyone could call the short clipped questions and answers that, was more an interview than small talk. Giselle got the distinct impression they were being graded on their performance. Only Di and Taylor seemed to be enjoying themselves. They'd spent most of dinner chatting up Ace and Jay. Those two reminded her of Asher, all formality at the front, but beneath the surface they were still kids, like her. Giselle wished Asher were there. He might have had a stick up his ass, but she could at least talk to him. And then it hit her: she'd rather have Asher than Damien.

Damien was her boyfriend. His easygoing nature and devilish smile were always enough to lighten the mood of any situation. Why then would she be hoping to have Asher around? Why was he even entering her thoughts?

Wolf. That was why. He was like her. He knew what it was like in the wolfy world. Witches had their own issues, but wolves were like a military unit, with all their rank and honor and duty. Only another wolf could truly understand and appreciate the true horror she'd felt sitting at the table with the big boy Alphas as she managed to do everything wrong.

Asher would never screw up, and just like in Harper's class, he'd have her back as she continued to muck up the night.

Damn it, though. She needed to get Asher out of her head. It felt like cheating the more she wanted to have him sitting next to her. But she *did* want him there, sitting next to her.

Bad Giselle! She buried the thought deep down, hoping it wouldn't surface again. Asher and Taylor were supposed to be a thing, and that went against the girl code to covet your BFF's or sister's man.

Damien. Damien. Damien. He was her boyfriend.

Giselle found herself panicking. All around her conversation was happening, talks of wolf politics, territory, potential mates to strengthen other regions, none of which she had any interest in. She was the outsider. In her mind, she was still the lone wolf, and no matter how much she wanted to fit into pack life, it didn't feel like she ever would.

"Please excuse me." Giselle stood and set her napkin down. "I'm not feeling well. I'm going to step outside for a little fresh air."

Martina's eyes struck Giselle like a target. She'd made the wrong move, but couldn't sit here in this awkwardness with her mind going a mile a minute any longer.

"You're not planning to go running, are you?" Martina's tone was dangerous. Not that Giselle expected any different. Her go to response to stress had always been a good run in the desert.

"No. I just need to step out and get a little air. I'll be back soon."

Martina nodded, and Giselle took the opportunity to sneak out the back sliding glass door.

Summer still burned the air, and even now, after the sun had set, the breeze prickled like hot cinders from an open flame, but that was less bothersome than the dinner or the absentee mother who'd just dropped into her lap. The timing couldn't have been worse. Why would the supreme wolf of wolves decide that now was the time to pay a visit? Unless. And it hit her like a ton of bricks. Cassandra had said that her potential father was some Alpha. What if her birth had pissed off more than just a witch coven? What if David was here checking up on her and the witch who had decided to show up out of the blue? It made sense. If they were pissed off enough, they might keep tabs. And Damien said the witch was no good and they were handling it. It was all starting to add up. Poor Cassandra had to be telling the truth. She'd wanted a baby, and because of it, she'd lost it all. Hated by the witches, hunted by the wolves. And she'd lost her daughter in the process. She had to go warn Cassandra. Had to at least give her that much.

The sliding glass door opened just as Giselle was about to break her promise to Martina. She stopped short of the back gate and before she could turn around, he spoke.

"Not running away, are you?" David's haughty tone mocked her more than his words could have.

"No. I just like to walk in the service alley. Fresh air and all," she lied, but closed the gate all the same.

"Of course. Lone wolves often cannot handle the formality of pack life. I bet I'm quite the thorn in your side tonight, am I right?" David sounded more congenial now than he'd been all night. The sudden shift piqued her interest.

She turned to face him. "Still learning my place. You know. Child of the system and all of that."

David nodded with a little "Um-hmm" as he stroked his beardless chin. "What do you know of your history?" he asked after a moment of reflection.

Giselle cursed under her breath. She'd been so close to leaving and avoiding this whole mess of a question. David had not taken his eyes off of her since they'd sat down to dinner, but she'd been warned to play nice, and had held her tongue. Now, being cornered like this with him asking questions she wasn't comfortable discussing set her teeth on edge.

"Nothing, really." She shrugged as if none of what she had to say carried any importance. "I was abandoned. Fostered, then adopted."

"That's is the short of it, isn't it?" He snickered, finally a genuine laugh of sorts, given the stick planted firmly up his ass. It lightened the mood between them enough for Giselle to feel comfortable taking a few steps closer to him. David crossed his arms and immediately regained his air of regality. "Where were you first taken in? Did your parents tell you?"

She'd had a set of parents until her first change had scared them half to death. At nine, she'd been sent back into the system, and been passed around Oregon like a hot potato until finally they'd sent her to Vegas. But she wasn't sure how much of that she wanted to tell David. "I didn't come from Vegas, if that's what you're asking."

"You're awfully defensive."

Understatement of the year, she nearly said, but chose to stick her foot even further in her mouth. "And you're kind of nosy." Giselle regretted it almost immediately.

David's eyes narrowed, his mouth forming a hard line of anger. The silence between them suddenly became deafening; even the crickets and cicada bugs had quieted, leaving only the screaming of her conscience telling her she'd overstepped this time.

Under the scrutiny of his angered glare, part of Giselle felt fear. He claimed to be their Regional leader, but she had no reason to respect him. She'd always been a lone wolf, and that mindset awarded no loyalty to anyone who had not earned it.

"I understand you are unfamiliar with our ways, so I'll let your disrespect slip this once, but you will have to learn your place." His eyes bore into hers.

She met his stare full on, her wolf rising to the surface, filling her with all the power she held within. "Respect is earned."

They stared locked for what felt like an eternity, and then small creases formed in David's brow. His eyes softened. "Very true, young Alpha. But remember it goes both ways."

She'd expected him to lash out. Her wolf was at the ready for a fight. She knew she'd have lost against a full grown male – she still had much to learn where fighting was concerned – but her strength of will went a long way. "I'm not comfortable with your line of questioning. My past is not a subject I like to think about, as it has not been pleasant."

"Now that is an acceptable answer." David nodded. "My interest in you has to do more with why and how you fell into the system, rather than you personally. It is not common for our kind to last long on our own. We need our packs."

She'd expected him to lash out. To impose his will as Alpha. But instead, he had responded with a more than fair and even tone, even commending her personal strength. Perhaps she had not given him the chance he deserved. Giselle considered it for a moment before revealing more of her past. "I came from Oregon. All over Oregon. My... condition... obviously caused problems."

"And your attitude as well, I bet." David chuckled again, another genuine laugh that showed in his eyes. Much less the creeper now, she understood his scrutinizing gaze to be more a part of his personality as Alpha.

She nodded. "I have been known to go my own way, yes."

"That's not safe for a young wolf."

"So I've been told many times."

"A good Alpha knows when to listen to the advice of others. It's not always about having your own will be done."

"Still learning that part."

"For a true Alpha, that is probably the hardest lesson of them all. It's easy to think you can do what you will, consequences be damned, but the reality is, without thought, actions are meaningless."

"I'll keep that in mind."

"No. You won't. You're placating me, hoping I'll end our conversation soon, so you can retreat to the safety of your sisters and recount all that you've gleaned from your time with me. Go. It's fine. They will be your council this evening. And some years down the line, my words will come back to you."

He'd nailed it. She was planning to do just that.

"Does this mean I'm free to go?" Giselle made a show of bowing to him.

"I'm not your enemy, despite what you may think. It is in my best interest to ensure the health and good care of all under my domain. Cases like yours are quite special, and as you no doubt guessed, fraught with problems. Humans don't want to know we exist, and we'd like to keep it that way too. That is why I asked what you know – so I can look into why it happened and help prevent it from happening again."

It all sounded good, and he was probably well intentioned, but she couldn't shake the feeling that there was more behind his questions than Alpha duty. She saw it in his eyes. There was a personal level to his line of questions as well. And if she had hit the nail on the head, it was Cassandra, and his desire to find and punish her for what she had done. That, she wouldn't allow.

"Like I said, I don't have much I can tell you. It was a blur of foster parents since my first change."

"If you do somehow remember something, please let me know. I will be here in Vegas until the end of the week."

Giselle nodded and walked past him back into the house. She'd text Cassandra at the very least and let her know the wolves were on to her.

11

Giselle had barely stepped into the house when Di ambushed her, snatching her up by the arms and dragging her into the kitchen. "You didn't embarrass the family just now, did you?" Di's whispered tone bordered on angry.

"What are you talking about?" Giselle asked.

"Shhhhh." Di pulled Giselle further into the kitchen, where they couldn't be seen. Others were enjoying after dinner coffee in the living room. "I saw the angry faces out there, you and David both. He's the Alpha's Alpha. You play nice with him."

There was no winning. Giselle might as well disappear for the rest of the week, because there was no way she could deal with this level of stress. "I was... sort of." She tried to pull out of Di's strong grip.

"Great." Di released Giselle, throwing up her hands in frustration. "Gavin was grinding his teeth all through dinner. Couldn't you hear it? And poor Martina. I mean, I have never seen her so stressed in my life."

"Why? It's not like we're in trouble." Giselle had never seen Di so worked up. The stress level in the whole house was at eleven, but Di was shaking as if she were about to go into full-on panic attack.

"Look. I've been here the longest. I've never met David before. He might have said this was some making the rounds kind of thing, but it's not, or I would have at least met him before. I was talking with Jay. They came directly to Vegas. No stopping to look around. And they have a meet and greet with the witch coven later this week. That's not normal."

"Did he say why?" Giselle asked, now more assured that her suspicion had been right. All the chips were falling into place, and with that, the small sense of certainty that she had a mother, a real live mother, began to take hold within her.

"He didn't come out and say why, but Jay told me that guy, Richard. You know, the silent Santa-looking guy?"

Giselle nodded.

"He's an enforcer. One of the guys that takes care of rule breakers."

"Martina and Gavin broke no rules." For the first time, Giselle felt a streak of panic. She wanted a mother, but not at the cost of her new family.

"No, of course they didn't." Di's word's had Giselle exhaling the biggest sigh of relief she'd ever given. "But that doesn't mean they aren't very concerned with why an enforcer was brought down. Wait... did *you* do something?"

"What the hell, Di!" Giselle said louder than she'd intended. She poked her head around the corner to see if she'd drawn any attention to their conversation, and when she was satisfied no one was really listening, she looked back at Di. "Seriously, you think I did something?"

"I'm just asking."

"So much for our sisterly bond."

"Oh, don't give me that bullshit. You know I love you and so does Taylor, but you are awfully secretive, and David paid no attention to either of us, but made the time to go outside for a private chat with you. What did he want to know?"

"He didn't talk to either of you?" Giselle was shocked. She'd been so stuck in her own head she hadn't even paid attention to what was going on around her.

"No. He was singularly focused on you. Why do you think Gavin is so stressed? Elle, if you have done something, tell me. Please."

"What could I have possibly done?"

"First Damien tells me to keep you occupied. Now the Mega Alpha is on your scent. Think."

"He asked about my birth and where I came from. That's it. And you know I don't know anything about that."

"What about that lady at Sammy's?"

Giselle shrugged, hoping to appear indifferent.

"She's a witch. She got you all riled up. And she's the reason Damien asked to keep you busy. Don't do this, Elle. We're a family. We're supposed to trust each other."

Di was right; she needed to put some faith in her pack and especially her new sisters. Giselle sighed, knowing she needed to tell her something but struggling with how much to say because she still hadn't sorted it all out in her own mind yet. "Fine. The lady at Sammy's says she knows me. Knows about my past. I want to find out more, but Damien says she's no good and that I should stay away." Giselle hoped that would be enough to sate Di's curiosity.

"Damien said she was bad and she couldn't be trusted." Di put her hands on Giselle's shoulders and met her eyes dead on. No animosity showed in her eyes, only concern matched by the plea in Di's voice. "Listen to him. I don't know what this lady is up to, but it sounds to me like she's trying to start trouble. Maybe that's why David is here."

"To take care of witch business? Not likely." Giselle shrugged out of Di's grip and backed away a step.

"Unless that witch is interfering in wolf business."

"By talking to a teenager?"

"Look. I don't know what her angle might be, but both sides are saying to stay out of it, so maybe listen for once?"

Giselle nodded. "You're right. Help me lie low for the week, then?" She hoped she sounded convincing enough. Di's heart was in the right place, and she didn't want start a fight, but there was no way she was staying out of things when she might be so close to learning about her true mother.

"Yes. We can start with helping Martina plan a party for our guests at the end of the week. They're supposed to do their dinner with Ash's family and meet the witches, but said their final evening will be here. Martina will need all the help she can get. We're hosting all the supernaturals here in the back yard."

Great. Just what she needed – a giant gathering of all the people she was supposed to be not pissing off. *That'll be totally fun.*

"And I assume Taylor is already upstairs planning our wardrobes?" Giselle asked.
"Of course. Now, let's go join her."

12

Compared to the abomination that had been the previous night's dinner, the thought of dealing with Mr. Harper first thing in the morning sounded absolutely pleasant.

As soon as Di pulled into the school's parking lot, even before she'd turned off the car, Giselle hopped out, coffee in hand, eager to experience the normalcy of teenage life with all its mundane drama. At least here, the worst Alpha she'd run into was a teacher, and their threats paled in comparison to teeth and claws of her kind's justice system.

She snatched up her bag and took a quick look across the parking lot, hoping to see a familiar face. Anyone not a wolf. She'd gladly spend an hour discussing the pros and cons of the latest zombie killer TV show if it meant a distraction from her own paranormal business. And just as that thought crossed her mind, she spotted Damien.

Not a wolf, sure, but not a normal kid either. *Damn*. Beggars couldn't be choosers.

"I'll catch up later, girls. Need to go talk to my man." She scurried across the parking lot and greeted Damien with a smile despite the early hour. "Thank the gods for coffee, right?"

He certainly looked as if he needed some. Small dark circles under his eyes said he'd been pulling some all-nighters, and since it was only the first week of school, that had to mean it was witchy business; another thing she'd rather not deal with at the moment. "Someone is in a better mood today." He swiped her cup and took a sip, cringing at the extreme sweetness, and immediately handed it back. "Damn. I'd be happy too with pure sugar flowing through my veins."

"Rocket fuel! Need a kick start some mornings." Giselle laughed and took a slug of her drink, enjoying the hot melted sugar.

"If I drank that, I'd be clawing the ceiling. How the hell do you sit still?"

"Wolfy secrets." Giselle winked.

"What other wolfy secrets are you hiding? My sources tell me—"

"Have you been spying on me?" Giselle snarled, her happy mood fading as quickly as it had come. She'd hoped the whole supernatural drama could wait until later, but clearly that was not in the stars. Not even 9 a.m., and she was right back into it again.

Despite her annoyed glare, Damien kept his cool, even turning an angry eye back at Giselle. "No. My coven has been watching Cassandra. And found you talking to her… twice. I thought you were going to lie low?"

Of course he'd been spying on her. That was strike two. And she'd thought she could trust him. As if their relationship might slant his loyalty toward her in some fashion. *No. Witch first.* That was becoming a painfully clear truth. No use beating around the bush with him, especially since he had spies all over the place checking in on her. "I really think she is my mother."

"She's not your mother." Damien shouted loudly enough to get the attention of other kids walking up the school steps.

"And you know this for a fact?" Giselle responded in kind.

He dropped his voice to a dangerous whisper. "I told you. Witches and wolves cannot have babies together."

"Cassandra seems to think otherwise," Giselle said.

"Oh and you're on a first name basis now, are you? Get it through your head: she's lying. She gave you a story." Giselle had never seen him so riled up. If he were a wolf, Damien might have sprouted a fur coat right there on the school steps. As it was, she felt the crackle of magic in the air. But that didn't deter her from her train of thought.

"Why would Cassandra lie to me?"

Damien shouldered his backpack and turned away, taking a deep breath as if needing to calm himself before speaking. "I don't know."

"And neither do I. That's the point. What reason would she have to lie to me about it? What could she possibly get out of claiming a stray wolf?"

"You make yourself sound like some lost puppy." Damien sighed and met her eyes, a bit calmer now, but still clearly bothered. "You know you're more important than that. You're going to be an Alpha someday. Everyone says it."

That word, Alpha, grated on her nerves. Who cared about being an Alpha? It was just a title to her. Leader of the pack. Big deal. She didn't need to be an Alpha. Not now. Not ever. She might be strong of will, but an Alpha was something she did not aspire to. "There are plenty of Alphas out there, none of which have anything to do with witches. Tell me, what does your family care who is the Alpha of either pack in the city here?"

Damien's lips pulled tight for a moment, as if he wanted to say something, but halted himself at the last second. Then he shrugged and shook his head.

"What was that?" Giselle asked.

His eyes grew wide. "What?"

"That thing you did. And your heart jumped when I asked about your family. What aren't you telling me?"

Damien shook his head. He couldn't hide the truth; his body language gave away more than he could ever say. But still he tried. "Nothing. I'm just... sick of what this woman is doing to you. Ever since she came here, she's had you all riled up. And with the Regional Alpha in town..."

Giselle rested her hands on her hips, narrowing her eyes as she watched him squirm with his half-truths. He was dangerously close to strike three with her. "I never mentioned the Regional Alpha."

"My... my mom mentioned it. You know she likes to keep an ear to the ground."

"Apparently so. What else does your mother tell you is happening? Do you know why they're here?"

Damien's heart jumped again, and his eyes dilated despite the bright morning light. He let out a slow breath and shrugged again. "I've told you all I know."

More lies. What a dick! "No. You haven't. And I don't like this new secretive version of you. What happened to my boyfriend? The guy who shared everything with me?"

"You know how it works in our families." He sighed again. "I share what I can, but there are some things I can't."

"Screw the family obligations. When it involves my family... you share."

"Sorry, Elle." He hung his head, avoiding her heated glare.

"Yeah. Me too." She turned away and walked up the steps without looking back.

How could he keep secrets from her? Especially when it directly affected her? Damien knew damn well why the Regional Alpha was in town. She pushed open the glass door so hard she nearly knocked it off the hinge and ran straight into Asher.

"We have got to stop meeting like this." Ash's large hands caressed her shoulders as he steadied her.

Giselle fought back the tears in her eyes and looked up to her friend, hoping he wouldn't see how close she was to losing it. "You and I will always be each other's punching bags, I fear," she said with a fake laugh to further hide her true emotions.

"You're probably right. Might as well make a career of it and become sparring partners." Asher threw a few quick jabs at her that didn't land. He gave her a little wink and then held his hands up as if waiting for her to fight back.

The lightness of his mood was infectious. Giselle pulled back her tears and took a cleansing breath. "Yeah. I could use a workout. Or maybe just a run." A run was exactly what she needed – to shed her human skin with all its problems and let the wolf take her into the wild where the wind could cleanse her soul.

"What's got you all riled up?" Asher asked.

"Nothing. Just..." *No, Giselle, don't start down that path. Breathe and calm yourself.*

"Boy trouble?" He threw an arm around her and guided her down the hallway towards their lockers.

"Do you know how old you sound when you say that?"

"I was going for funny. I heard you like that in a guy. Worked for Damien."

"Yeah, keyword... *worked.*" Just hearing his name at that moment had her hackles up again.

Asher must have sensed it. He stopped short and pulled away from her. "Wow. I thought I was the only one who could make you that mad. He must have done something pretty bad."

The concern in his voice warmed her heart. They'd been friends since she'd started school here, despite their rocky start, and though he had a stick up his ass regarding rules and duty, Asher was the closest thing to a best friend she could have. At times she wondered if it would have worked out for them if they'd had the chance to become something more. He matched her in all the ways that were important and balanced her in everything else. But he was off limits. Taylor had claim to him. And that was a rule even she wouldn't break.

Ash's eyes begged her to explain what was causing her such obvious pain. *Damien.* But this was one area she knew she shouldn't lean on him for support. Relationships were something that crossed the friend line.

"I can't talk to you about that." Giselle continued walking down the hall, knowing Asher would follow.

"Then find a subject you can talk about, and let's go for a walk." He took her hand, pulling her backwards toward the door.

Giselle shook her head, standing her ground in the middle of the busy hallway, forcing kids to walk around her to get to their classes. "We'll miss chem."

"That's not really a convincing argument against my plan," Asher said, with his trademark wink. He could be devilishly charming when he wanted, and Giselle was *this close* to saying yes.

"You're supposed to be the good wolf... remember?" she laughed.

Asher scrunched his face in mock anger. "Okay, fine. We won't skip class. But after school, you and I are going for a run, okay?"

"Now that I could do." Giselle smiled and took Ash's arm, pulling him down the hall with her. "Have you had your visit with the Alphas?"

To outsiders they might have looked like a couple, walking arm and arm, and Giselle could see a few curious looks followed by whispers that would become rumor.

"Not yet. We're due tomorrow." Asher didn't seem bothered in the slightest by the nosy onlookers. Giselle wondered if Damien were there, in the shadows watching, and part of her hoped he was, seeing her with Asher... happy. *That would serve him right.*

"Why are they here?" Giselle asked, with genuine curiosity. She'd already gotten mixed signals from the previous night's dinner, and if anyone knew about rules and regulations, it was the Thrace pack.

"They're looking for something," Asher responded, with refreshingly blunt truth. "That much I know. But they aren't coming out and saying it. I heard they have a meeting with the witches tonight."

"That's odd, isn't it?"

"Yeah. We normally keep out of each other's politics, but they seemed very eager to meet with the local coven," Asher said.

Finally someone who would lay it all out there. No subtext. No hidden agenda. Ash's words, though bringing up more questions in her mind, were a comfort to her. At least she knew she could trust him. "I wonder if it has to do with the new witch in town," Giselle said, offering up her own truth to the conversation.

"There's a new witch?"

"Damien spotted her a couple days ago at Sammy's."

Asher shook his head and shrugged. "Transient town. And besides, that shouldn't matter much to the Alphas."

"Damien seemed to think she was important." Why was she speaking his name? Every time she said it, she felt pangs of anger and sadness equally.

"I'm sure it will all blow over in a day or two. The Alphas rarely go on tour, so after they leave, it could be years before we see them again." Asher sounded as if this visit were really not as interesting as her family had made it seem.

"Where do they live?" She continued to fish for more information since he alone seemed willing to give it.

"Somewhere in Washington. Not really sure."

"D.C.?"

"Nah. State. They have to live in their territory, silly."

"Can't blame a girl for being confused. Remember, I'm still a newbie to all this pack business."

"You are such a noob," Asher teased. "But don't be bothered by it. As long as no one steps out of line, like causing some newsworthy werewolf sighting, the Alphas are more like monarchs. They like to parade around, wave at people, enjoy the bowing and scraping; but other than that, they have no bearing on day-to-day pack business. Just worry about your family pack."

They sounded more and more like the kind of people Giselle couldn't stand to be around. All the pompous arrogance that went with inherited titles. Another reason she'd rather never have the title and responsibility of being a pack Alpha. "We don't have to pay tribute or anything to them, do we?"

"There's the ritual sacrifice of your firstborn.... But that's years away."

Giselle laughed and slapped at Ash's arm. "You don't do the funny thing very well. Just saying."

"Wow... I'm hurt. Really."

"Somehow I doubt anything could hurt you. You're way too self-assured."

"That's true." Asher puffed his chest and looked over her head with a faux gaze of arrogance. "I know I am the shit. Bow before my majesty."

She tried to hold back her laugh and snorted in the process. He was such a straight man most days, and then he'd surprise her with random glimpses of this other truly funny side of himself. "You just keep telling yourself that. Someday it might come true." Giselle walked into Mr. Harrison's class wearing a smile put there by Asher, and as fast as she let the feeling wash over her, a small voice in the back of her mind made her feel that it was somehow wrong.

13

Heart and mind warring with each other, compounded by the fact that when she was finished with her day of mundane school life, wolfy politics awaited her, had the day dragging by at a snail's pace.

The bright light at the end of the tunnel was her date to go running with Asher.

Wait. Not a date, she had to remind herself. *Not a date. Just two friends. Two wolf friends, doing what wolves do – burning off a little energy out in the desert.*

Running was the important part; letting the hot breeze of the desert blow through her fur. Maybe she'd catch a jackrabbit or two. They were always good fun. That's all this was.

So why was she having to convince herself so hard that this was all it was?

Ash's warm smile and playful attitude clung to her memory like a ghost with unfinished business, while anger and resentment at Damien soured her mood.

But despite her anger at Damien, a small voice of reason nudged her toward understanding. Damien was a witch, and just like she was a wolf, loyalty came to family or pack first.

Relationship or no relationship, family was what took precedence.

And yet, Asher had been more truthful with her than Damien had. He had nothing to gain from it, either. He just offered up what he knew without hesitation.

What could the witches be hiding that was so bad it had to be kept from Giselle? And why, if Giselle was learning information from Cassandra, was it imperative to continue the veil of secrecy? They'd have to know it would only push her closer and closer to Cassandra.

The more she thought about it, the angrier she got. And the angrier she got, the more she studied the clock, watching the second hand refuse to move faster and let her get to what she wanted most: running.

By the time the final bell rang for school, she was like a predator in hot pursuit, running full speed to the parking lot in search of Ash's truck.

Of course she beat him there, and then had to endure the seemingly endless flow of students pouring out of the front doors and down the stone steps like a flood to clog the parking lot.

Asher trickled out, the last drop in the rushing tide, moving with the urgency of a sloth.

"You want walk slower there, Thrace?" she called out to Asher, whose vacant expression said he'd forgotten about their plans.

The hope of a good run had been the only thing keeping her from the edge of sanity all day. She'd hoped he had the same desire, but clearly she'd been wrong.

"Feisty today." He laughed and unlocked the truck. "You must really need to blow off some steam."

"You don't even know the half of it." Giselle slid inside and started removing her shoes.

"Whoa there, lady, you going to shift here and hang your head out the window while I drive?" Asher laughed.

"The thought had occurred to me."

She'd have done it, too, just to get a rise out of him, but it seemed all it took were words to have his chin nearly hit the ground as his eyes threatened to bulge out of their sockets. Giselle giggled at his expression as it turned from shock to annoyance. Mr. Rules and Regulations came back with a vengeance not two seconds later. "Well, don't. That shit will get us in trouble."

His sharp tone only made her laugh more. "Okay."

While his expression softened toward her, his jaw remained tight as he looked past her.

"It was only a joke," Giselle started to say, but cut herself short watching wrinkles appear at his brow. "Everything okay?"

Asher shook himself from whatever it was stealing his attention and looked down at Giselle. "Sorry. We have company."

It was Giselle's turn to look confused. She glanced behind her, not sure of what to expect, and spotted two guys she'd only just met, walking right towards them.

For a moment worry had her by the throat, but she remembered the way the Alpha's sons were so very similar to Asher and how she'd wanted him to meet them at last night's dinner. "That's Ace and

Jay," she said with a smile. They'd laughed and joked and genuinely tried to be friendly, whereas their father had just been a creeper. Couldn't hold it against them. And Di had seemed really cozy with Jay by the end of the night; so, really, they couldn't have been all bad.

"Who?"

"The Regional Alpha's boys."

"Shit. Really?" Asher began straightening his shirt and used the mirror to check his appearance. Giselle laughed, seeing him primping and preening. For the first time in probably ever, he reminded her of Taylor.

"Don't be such a girl. They're cool." Giselle turned around to greet them. "Hey, guys!"

The taller of the two, Ace, smiled back and offered his hand to shake. Giselle took it on instinct and was caught off guard when he pulled her out of the truck straight into a bear hug.

"Giselle, right? Dad's been going on and on about you, the big mystery girl," Jay said with a little flirty wink. "We might need to get to know you a little better."

Heat rushed to her cheeks. What a flirt. And cute, too. She could have fun getting to know him and his brother a little better too.

Ace released Giselle from the bear hug, but kept his arm around her as if they were old friends. His odd familiarity should have put her off, but she kind of enjoyed it.

Asher walked around his truck to where Giselle and the guys were standing. He looked as if he were going to grind his teeth into dust watching the way the guys were flirting with her. She'd never seen him so protective before. Not that she needed protecting; these guys were wolfy royalty. They'd no sooner step out of line than Asher would, for fear of good old dad's retribution. But it was nice to see that he regarded her so closely.

"Oh, guys. This is Ash," Giselle started to say.

"Yeah, we know. Thrace, right? We get to party with you guys in a couple days." Jay was the one to extend his hand this time, and for the briefest of moments, Asher looked as if he wanted to bite it off rather than accept it.

"Good to meet you," Asher said stiffly.

"Don't mind him." Giselle pushed away from Ace's body. "We were just about to go on a run. You know, blow off some steam. That kind of thing."

"Any good *run* spots out here?" Jay asked, emphasizing the word *run* as if he had some ulterior meaning.

Giselle rolled her eyes. Guys. Always thinking with their little heads. "We have some open desert leading to the Sheep Mountains out behind my neighborhood."

"Nice," Ace said. "A little quiet patch of desert for some *running*."

No use trying to correct them again. Whatever. Let them have their innuendo. As long as she was able to get out and do some actual running, they could joke all they wanted to about what they thought was going to happen.

"Did you want to run with us?" Asher asked politely, but his tone clearly said they were not welcome.

"Naw. We can't interrupt your running time." Jay winked at Asher and then smiled sweetly at Giselle. "Anyway, we're supposed to hang with your sisters for a little. You know where they are?"

Giselle let out a sigh of relief. She hadn't ever seen Asher so riled up. And there was no real reason for it. The guys were just being friendly, albeit a little too flirty. It was obvious they had a one-track mind. But knowing they were not joining made all the difference.

She looked across the parking lot, spotting Di just walking down the stairs. "There's Di. Taylor won't be too far behind. Where you guys off to?"

Jay shrugged. "Not sure. Maybe we'll get in a little run time ourselves. We'll definitely be in good company."

Giselle snorted. Not likely. If they thought they were getting anything from Di and Taylor except a makeover, they were barking up the wrong tree. But Giselle wouldn't say that out loud. She'd let them learn their fate in due time. She just shook her head. "You guys go have fun. Ash and I have to run." She played along with the joke, giving Jay a flirty wink of her own. "I'll see you around again, right?"

Ace smiled slyly at Asher. "Good luck, man."

Jay regarded Giselle with curiosity for a moment. "Oh, we'll definitely see you again. We have to learn more about the mystery wolf."

"Not much I can tell you guys. Your dad knew more of my story than I did." She nervously giggled.

Jay started walking towards the stairs. "Okay, then. We'll let you two have your *run*. Stay safe and out of sight."

Ace pulled Giselle in for one more hug and followed his brother out across the parking lot.

"I don't like them," Asher half-whispered, half-growled.

Giselle laughed. His protectiveness was endearing, even if it was misguided. The guys were standard issue boys. Flirting was the name of the game, and why not? No harm in being playful. "Be nice. I didn't like you when I first met you, either."

"They're players. Just look at them."

Giselle looked across the parking lot and saw Jay with his arm around Taylor just as it had been around her a few minutes before. And Ace was getting in close with Di.

She shrugged. "They're like princes, I guess. Of course they're going to be cocky and self-assured. That works in their favor."

"Don't tell me you like them." Asher continued his grumpfest.

"I don't care either way. They're here for a couple of days, and then they'll be gone. They haven't done anything to piss me off, so why hate on them?"

Asher shrugged.

"You're jealous because Ace is over there with Taylor, aren't you?" Giselle asked, breaking her own rule of not crossing the friend zone line with talk of relationships.

"Just drop it. We have a run to go on, right?" Asher got back into his truck and turned the engine on.

"I don't like fake people. And they are as fake as it comes. Lording around because they're sons of the Regional Alpha. One of them will be our Alpha one day, and I would rather it be someone with a little more class."

Giselle huffed. "We're all a bunch of kids, remember? Now's the time to be young and stupid, not to stress about all that leadership crap." Wow.

Mr. Rules and Regulation was back in full force, and she remembered why he grated on her nerves sometimes. The stick was planted firmly up his ass now, and she hoped that after a little run, he might work it loose – before he sent her running off alone. The last thing she needed was more wolfy drama; she'd already had her fill of that.

Asher growled. "In my family, we must be respectful of our position and that of the position of those above us. There's no room for stupid kid stuff."

"Jeez, chill, okay? Let's get our run in and blow off this steam. I'm not trying to fight with you."

They rode in silence all the way to the spot where they could shift in solitude and take off on paws.

14

Nature's cleansing breath had worked its magic again, gently caressing the troubles away as Giselle sprinted through the dry brush and bounded over large rocks in the desert skirting the mountain's edge. Asher could hardly keep up, she ran with such purpose and seemingly endless energy. Her intention was to run until her legs could not, burning away the stress and doubts clinging to her mind.

Hours might have gone by; time had lost all meaning. Out there in the open land, her spirit was free. Not for the first time in her life, she wondered if simply staying wolf would be the better choice. Life – the human version of it – held more complications than it was worth. Boy troubles, family obligations, supernatural crap... how the hell was she supposed to make sense of all of that? Life spent as a foster kid with nothing but human parents who didn't want her had not prepared her for the other side of the coin. Belonging was proving to be even harder than being a loner.

More than once, Asher yipped at her, probably wanting her to slow down and wait for him, but the call of the wild held her captive, and she ran until she could no longer.

Panting and out of breath, Giselle felt better than she had all week. Trotting back toward the truck, she shifted back to her human form and grabbed her clothes out of the back of Ash's truck.

"You've gotten faster," Asher said, pulling his pants up behind the hood of the truck.

"I needed to run." Giselle let out a satisfied breath. Muscles aching and heart pounding, her wolf had burned through all its pent up energy, and with that her sprit was finally at peace.

"I know it's not my place – Damien should be here talking to you – but I want you to know I'm here for you. I can see you're bothered by something. I'm not even going to pry. But I'm your friend." He hesitated when he said it. "I care about your stubborn ass."

"You care about my ass?" Giselle laughed.

"Who wouldn't?" He playfully whipped his t-shirt at her.

"Was that you trying to flirt?"

"Depends on if it worked or not." Asher winked. "Ace and Jay seemed to have some game with you." Jealousy still colored his tone where those two boys were concerned.

"I don't get you. You're Mr. Aloof all the time, and then you go and flirt with me, knowing full well I have a boyfriend."

"A boyfriend you seem to be angry with. What did he do?"

"You said no prying."

Asher held up his hands in surrender. "Right. I did. Well, then, I guess I'm guilty on both counts."

Giselle finished dressing and sat on the tailgate of Ash's truck. "No one did anything, really. Life is just complicated, that's all. We come from different worlds."

He walked around and took a spot next to Giselle on the tailgate, sending the truck dipping slightly under his weight. "Witches are different, that's for sure."

"It's not even that. Deep down, I'm still a lone wolf. Don't get me wrong – I love my family. And I love my friends. But I know the only person I can truly trust with one hundred percent certainty is myself."

"Damn. That's harsh."

"I don't mean for it to sound so bad, but really, do you blame me? I spent 16 years being passed around from family to family, always hoping they would be the one. Now I have a good one and I love them to death. But there are still secrets and things I have yet to learn. I didn't even know there was a Regional Alpha until yesterday and he cornered me to ask about my past. Where was my new family to save me from that? Actually, they were a bit pissed at me for not behaving better. As if I should know by instinct what to do."

"Take a breath. Your heart is racing." Asher placed a steadying hand on Giselle's shoulder. "I hear you."

"You know, I believe you."

"Why me?"

"Because from the very beginning, even when you were being a dick, you tried to be honest with me. Remember when you warned me about Martina?"

"But I was wrong about them. My family..."

"My point is, you tried to warn me with information you felt was right. No one else would tell anything me until I pried it out of them, but you came forward."

"I'm the good guy, okay? Let's go with that." Asher flashed her that disarming smile that could make any girl melt, and Giselle was no less affected by it. She allowed her heart to slow and released the tension she'd been holding onto.

"So if I'm the only one you can trust, tell me what's got you all bent out of shape," Asher said.

Giselle let her shoulders slump and turned away, not wanting to see Ash's face as she said, "I want to know who my mother is and where I come from."

"You think the Regional Alphas know?" There was more than a little suspicion in his tone, his voice betraying any attempt he might have made to rein in his curiosity.

"I do. But they won't say. Their leader, David, he was too interested in me for just a simple family visit. And I didn't want to say anything to my sisters. They were too concerned with how much I was embarrassing them by not being a proper little werewolf."

Asher sat quietly for a few minutes as if in deep contemplation, but Giselle knew better; he just couldn't come up with anything else to say. Maybe he was in on it too? Maybe she was wrong in her assumption that he could be trusted with her secret curiosity.

"Or maybe I'm just overthinking things. I mean, I was in the system for a long time. Probably longer than most werewolves ever. I'm an oddity."

"Yes, you are most certainly odd," Asher laughed.

"It would be nice to know where I came from."

"I can't pretend to know how that feels. But I do envy you having spent time away from pack life. It does get a bit..."

"Stifling. Tedious. Repressive..."

"I was going to go with *ordinary*, but apparently you find it a bit worse."

In her own downward spiral of unease, she had somehow managed to insult Asher. She should have known better than to speak so harshly. He lived by all that stifling oppression. The rigidity of pack life suited him. "I didn't mean it like that."

"Sure sounded that way."

Giselle sighed, feeling more and more as if she should just take off into the desert and stay a wolf. She hadn't meant to step on Ash's feelings, and yet here they were, and he sounded totally butt-hurt. "I love my family. I guess I'm just still learning my place in the grand scheme of things."

"We're still kids; we're supposed to have rules and order, you know."

"How old are you again?"

"Old enough to know when I should be the responsible one. You're acting like a brat, Giselle. My family is ten times more restrictive than yours. It sucks sometimes, but you know what, I can count on my family for anything. I know my place, and I know they've got my back."

"Being a lone wolf has just given me a different perspective; but yeah, you're right. I am being a brat."

"Good. Now go home and enjoy the fact that you have one to go to."

"Yes, sir."

"Don't call me *sir*. I'm not my father."

"Could have fooled me." She jabbed him lightly in the rib.

"Oh, you wanna go, do you?" Asher grabbed Giselle by the hand and pulled her off the tailgate, spinning her around so his hand crossed her body, pulling her in tight against his chest. "I may not be my father, but I'm Alpha enough to take you on."

She shouldn't have enjoyed the way her body fit up against Ash's or the fact that his small show of dominance had her heart racing. She was with Damien. Not Asher. But part of her, the wolf, recognized that kindred spirit and desired that connection.

Silence passed between them. Ash's chest rose and fell with unusually labored breath. Giselle heard the kick of his heart beating faster than it had moments before, and she wondered what thoughts might be going through his head.

"Okay, Alpha. I submit." Giselle kept her tone light, though she was giddy and bubbling over with an excited rush.

"Can I get that in writing? The great Alpha-to-be Giselle submits to Asher Thrace." He let her go and Giselle spun to face him.

"Nope." She winked and turned to climb into the passenger seat of Ash's truck.

"Had to try. One of these days…"

"Only in your wildest of dreams. Now take me home." Giselle slammed the door closed.

15

"Oh, good. You're home." Taylor caught Giselle as she was walking up the drive to the house. "We're kidnapping you."

Taylor snatched Giselle by the arm and backed her towards the car. Di walked out of the house like a woman on a mission and unlocked the car with her remote.

"What's the occasion this time?" Giselle asked, wondering if they were being sisterly or doing as Damien suggested and occupying her time.

"No homework tonight, and I am starving for some good food," Di said, as she scooted into the driver's seat.

"Where are Ace and Jay?" She asked.

"Had to do dinner with the pack," Di said nonchalantly.

"And your double date... do I get details?" Giselle asked.

"Nope. Right now, we find food. Good food," Di responded.

Giselle couldn't tell if Di was happy or upset about their time spent with the Silverman boys. The fact that she was ready to scarf down some food though was clue enough that she was feeling stressed, and that was something Giselle needed to get to the bottom of. "Fine. What defines good food?" Giselle asked curiously.

"Something that covers all the major food groups: greasy, salty, fattening, and chocolate," Di said.

Yeah, Di was definitely stressing about something. But those were Giselle's favorite food groups too. Who could resist? "You won't get any complaint from me there. I just finished a run. I'm starving," she said.

"Yeah... um. What's with you running with Ash?" Taylor's tone left nothing to the imagination. Something was up between them, and it wasn't good.

"Do we not like Ash this week?" Giselle asked, hoping a lighter tone might smooth things over.

Taylor's lip curled, but when she spoke she kept her voice neutral. "Just wondering. You guys are awfully chummy lately."

Had she misread something? Breaking the girl code was not her style at all. If she'd had even the slightest inkling that hanging with Asher was going to cause a problem, she'd never have asked him to run. "Tay, seriously. If I'm interfering in your relationship, just say. You're my—"

"Nope. Do whatever you will." Taylor cut her off. "I don't really care. I just think it's odd you aren't with Damien."

Taylor was a terrible liar. But her message had been received loud and clear. Asher was in the no fly zone. "Well, Damien has witchy business to attend to, doesn't he? I mean, he did tell you to both to keep me busy without so much as clueing me into what is going on." Giselle hadn't meant to sound so bitchy, but Damien was a sore subject at the moment. Probably just as sore as Asher was for Taylor.

The car fell silent for a few awkward moments before Di spoke up. "See? This is why we are having a girls' night. Stupid boys! Asher and Damien are not to be mentioned for the rest of the evening, okay?"

"Screw the boy drama," Taylor eagerly agreed.

Giselle saw it for what it was – a way to ensure that Damien's plan was effective. Can't pry for info or go looking where she shouldn't if she's locked into girls' night with her sisters adamant about keeping all boy talk silent. But the idea of a night with no guy bullshit was just what they needed. "Whatever." Giselle shrugged.

"Don't be stubborn, Elle. You've been a real bitch lately, you know. Stop it," Di said.

Giselle stuck her tongue out at the back of Di's head. "And you both are perfect rays of sunshine all the time?"

"See, I knew she would do this," Taylor groaned.

Giselle took a breath. Maybe she was being a bit harsh with her sisters. "Sorry. Let's go stuff our faces with something deep fried and covered in chocolate."

"That's what I'm talking about." Di laughed. She drove toward their favorite pizza place, Sammy's.

For a weeknight the place was pretty busy, but they were becoming a staple there, and the waiter found them a booth with hardly any wait time.

Across the room, Giselle spotted a familiar face: Cassandra, sitting alone at a table, eating a salad. She remembered she hadn't yet sent the warning text to her about the Alphas' and the witches' meeting. She slid her phone out of her pocket and fumbled with it, making sure Di and Taylor were busy with the menu, and sent a quick note to Cassandra.

Giselle: *Witches and Wolves meeting tonight. You're suspicious to them.*

As if the woman could sense her presence, she looked up and spotted Giselle. Her eyes flitted to the two girls and then down to her phone on the table.

Cassandra: *Am I still suspicious to you?*

Giselle found herself smiling as she read the text.

"Hey. No boys, remember? Put the phone away." Taylor reached to grab her phone, but Giselle was quicker and slid it back into her pocket.

"How do you know I was texting a boy?" she responded.

"Um, that goofy grin on your face. Does this mean you and Damien have forgiven each other? Because seriously, I can't stand this new bitchy Elle," Di remarked.

"Damien and I are fine," Giselle lied. Better they think she was forgiving him than know what was truly going on.

"Which we all know is girl speak for 'That asshole better show up with some chocolates the next time he sees me'," Di said.

"Couldn't hurt." Giselle shrugged and picked up her menu with the guise of looking for something to eat, but just above the edge of the laminated tri-folded paper she could see Cassandra staring at her. She wished telepathy were a real thing at that moment because if she kept that up, people were going to notice. Her phone buzzed in her pocket and she snuck it out, holding it behind the menu.

Cassandra: *They know about me. And they aren't telling you the real reason they took you out. The Alphas are meeting with your parents as well.*

Suspicion grew like a weed. Martina was a stickler for family dinners, especially during the school week. *Why had she let the girls go out tonight?*

"I will take that phone if you keep this up." Di snatched the menu down, busting Giselle as she stared straight into the small screen."

Giselle snarled. "Try, and I'll break your hand."

"Okay. That's it." Di stood, slamming her own menu on the table. "I'm trying. Really trying, Elle, but you're making it impossible."

"To what? Keep secrets from me? Martina was totally okay with us missing dinner tonight? Why did you really bring me out here?"

The look on Di's face said it all. She could play angry all she wanted, but the truth was, everyone was doing their best to keep Giselle occupied and out of wolf and witchy business. "Okay, yeah. Martina and Gavin were a little worried you might be better off not joining dinner tonight because they're out with the other Alphas."

"So why not just come out with it?" Giselle asked angrily.

"Because you're being all super suspicious and bitchy about everything. I'd rather just gloss over the whole thing and enjoy a free meal out on Gavin's credit card," Taylor said, with a surprising measure of annoyance. She was normally the soft-spoken one, and hearing her as riled up as she was struck a chord with Giselle.

"I can't argue with that," Giselle said, hoping to lighten the mood. "And I'm intending to order something expensive just because."

"But you can argue with us about every other freaking thing these days," Di said, refusing to let the subject go.

Giselle's phone buzzed again. She glanced down seeing another message from Cassandra.

Cassandra: *Tell them about me. It will be a good test of their friendship.*

"What the hell? Who keeps messaging you?" Di snatched at the phone, but Giselle's reflexes were quicker, and she was able to keep it out of her sister's reach.

"Fine. You want to put an end to all this argu-ing?" Giselle said. She hoped she was doing the right thing. Across the room, Cassandra sat with an angelic smile on her face, silently urging her mes-sage to be told.

Di huffed and sat. "And how do we do that?"

"Honesty. Real, true, honesty. We're supposed to be sisters, right? That goes beyond pack," Giselle said, staring down Di with all the power of her Alpha wolf.

Surprisingly, Di shrugged rather than rise to the challenge. "Sure. Whatever."

"Don't be so flippant. That's why I can't trust you," Giselle said.

"Then trust *me*," Taylor said. She at least sounded sincere.

"See that woman across the way?" Giselle pointed to Cassandra.

"Yeah. That's the witch that's causing all the pack trouble," Taylor said.

"I need to know all you know about her," Giselle said.

"She's rogue. No coven. Apparently she's been in hiding for something like 16 years for messing with the mind of the Regional Alpha's brother." Di fiddled with her menu as if it were more interesting than their conversation.

Her reluctance to look at Cassandra properly and the odd way she backed down from Giselle's challenge had her questioning how much more was being unsaid.

"What do you mean, messing with his memories?" Giselle demanded.

"You know that whole magical contract thing? The one you always joke with me about because of Damien?" Di said, still refusing to look Giselle in the eye.

"Yeah. Sure."

"It's a real thing. She was involved in some witchy business with David's brother, and it went south. The brother is vegetable now. And she's suspected of being the witch who made him that way," Di continued.

Not the revelation she'd expected to hear; and not the story Cassandra had told her either. And she'd been alone with that woman twice now. Her mind played out all kinds of scenarios where she could have ended up a frog or worse at the hands of the redheaded woman she'd been so close to calling mother. "Really? How do they know it's her?" Giselle gave up all intention of revealing Cassandra to be her potential mother now.

Across the room Cassandra ate her salad, casting quick glances at the girls as they talked.

"If it is her," Di leaned in and whispered, "she's got a tribal wolf tattoo baying at the moon goddess on the back of her neck. It's a mix of the symbols for the coven she used to belong to and the wolf pack David comes from. She was like their liaison."

"If they know it's her, why are they not coming after her?" Giselle asked. "Why not just swoop in and grab her? It's not like she's got bodyguards." She thought back to the first time she'd seen Cassandra – there had been two guys with her the first night. And she hadn't seen them since. A chill ran down her spine. Something must have happened to them. More questions flooded her brain. More doubts and worries. Mother or not, this woman carried some heavy baggage, and it seemed no one had a straight story to tell about her.

"That's probably what they're all meeting about: the proper way to do things. You know how it is with us supernaturals. We have rules and stuff," Di said.

"I get that, but if someone is a wanted criminal, might be best to take them in for questioning before they get a chance to sneak away," Giselle said.

"They know you're sneaking around with her. They're trying to find the best way to bring her in safely because no one wants you getting hurt," Taylor jumped in, still sounding as annoyed as before.

Giselle met her eyes, finding not concern but jealousy, as if she had intentionally brought all this attention on herself. She hadn't. She'd never asked for the spotlight, and would much rather just live out her life the way she'd been doing. It was this woman, Cassandra, who had invaded her world and turned it upside down, bringing all the drama of the witches and the wolves down upon her while earning the ire of her sisters in the process.

"So, I've told you my part. Now, why is she so important to you?" Di asked.

"Because she keeps following me. Thinks I'm important to her somehow. I asked Damien about it, and he got all secretive on me. And then you all have been too. Everywhere I go this lady is there. And it's getting me into all this trouble." Giselle hoped her sisters would see how stressed out she'd been over this whole witch business and stop hating on her for it.

"You need to tell Martina, like now. If she truly is the witch they think she is, you could be in danger," Taylor said, finally dropping the attitude and sounding more like her normal self.

"Yeah," Giselle nodded. "I'll talk to Martina tonight.

"Okay. Good. Now can we put all this drama behind us and eat?" Di asked.

"Not sure if I want to with that woman staring at us," Giselle said.

Giselle didn't need to tell Di twice; she was on her feet and already taking a step toward the door. "Okay, fine. Let's go somewhere else."

Giselle's phone buzzed again, but this time she refused to look at it and followed her sisters out to the car.

16

The girls settled on eating at the food court in the mall, so everyone could pick something they liked and finish off the evening with their favorite pastime – shopping!

With the drama finished, for the most part, the girls settled into their old routine of talking about fashion, makeup, and even though it had been labeled taboo, boys played a huge part in their verbal agenda.

Di had been interested in Ace, and after their short hangout with the boys earlier in the day, her interest had gone to full-blown crush level.

Giselle stuffed her face full of the biggest and greasiest hamburger she could find: a triple decker with cheese and all the trimmings. A side of onion rings and a shake completed her meal, and even after she at that, she eyeballed a cinnamon bun, debating whether or not she should.

Taylor had chosen somewhat healthier options, going with a plain chicken sandwich and a fruit cup. Even pigging out, that girl managed to pick the lamest of options.

Di hardly ate her own meal; she spent the whole time talking about Ace.

Hearing about Di's love life for a change was a relief for Giselle and it seemed Taylor as well. They sat with earnest interest, listening to Di go on and on about the future she'd envisioned as potential princess of the packs, mated to Ace.

Giselle laughed to herself, wondering if Ace would be Alpha enough to deal with Di. She and her sister butted heads regularly, and even Giselle had a hard time with Di's level of dominance.

It was just what the girls needed to unwind and connect again as sisters, and by the time they headed home, Giselle had considered revealing the rest of the story about Cassandra to them. But as they pulled into the driveway, Di reminded Giselle of her talk with Martina, and like the curtain dropping after a show, the stress and worry slammed down, nearly crippling Giselle's mood.

The last thing she wanted to do was keep her word about talking to Martina. She wasn't even sure what she would say or reveal about the woman who was claiming to be her mother, especially after hearing what she'd done to another wolf.

But as soon as they walked through the door, Di called out, "Martina, Giselle needs to talk to you," and stood there like a sentry waiting for Giselle to unload her new information.

So much for their newfound sense of camaraderie.

Taylor took her place next to Di, crossing her arms in front of her, and locked eyes on Giselle as if waiting for the monologue to start.

Being in the spotlight was not how Giselle had envisioned this talk going, and it further added to her mounting stress over all the supernatural crap this week. She was just about ready to tell them off when Martina strolled into the living room. Hair up in a mom-bun, wearing a matching set of pink pajamas, she looked as if she'd been moments from going to bed.

"What's going on?" Martina asked lazily. No doubt tired after dealing with the other pack and the wolves, Martina yawned and set herself heavily on the sofa.

"Di thinks we need to have a talk." Giselle tried to sound as if it were no big deal.

"Do I need to go all den mother on someone? Damien giving you trouble?" Martina might have been joking, but Giselle had seen her invoke the Alpha. She could be one scary lady.

"No.... I just..." Giselle looked back at Di and Taylor, still standing there, all eyes and ears.

Martina pointed a finger toward the stairs and shook her head. "I'll talk to her alone, girls. You go upstairs."

Thankfully, neither Di nor Taylor would disobey the direct order of their Alpha. Shoulders slumping, the two girls slowly walked up stairs.

Martina turned her attention to Giselle.

If she could have ran away, Giselle would have. She didn't even know where to begin.

"Something is bothering you, I can tell." Martina stared her down with all the power of her Alpha wolf behind her. "Now, we're going to sit here for as long as it takes for you to tell me all about it."

"I don't want to talk." The truth in that statement could not be emphasized any more, but it would not save her from having to do just that. Already Martina's scrutinizing eyes were boring into her face, searching for body language clues to match with her tone. Her wolf hearing would be zeroing in on her heartbeat to see if she was lying. Pulling the wool over your parents' eyes took on a whole new level of difficulty when those parents were wolves. She didn't want to have to lie or give false information, but deep in her heart she felt something was wrong. Whether it was what the girls had told her or what Cassandra had said, she didn't know, but she couldn't allow herself to condemn someone until she felt she had it right.

"You might not want to talk, honey, but the last time you kept secrets from us, you went out and got yourself torn to shreds." Martina's tone turned serious.

Giselle's cheeks flushed with embarrassment. Martina was right. But she couldn't find the words she needed to express herself properly.

"Come on. Sit." Martina patted the spot next to her on the couch.

Giselle sighed and took a seat. "When you adopted me... how much information did the state give you?"

"I'd hoped this conversation would come later. What's brought this on?" Martina asked.

"Nothing really," she lied, and could hear her own heart betray her with sudden acceleration. "I just still have blank spots in my past. I had to have come from somewhere before I got put into the system."

"I don't believe that for a second. Something has riled you. Was it David and his entourage?"

Giselle's heart raced. There was no way she could get through this conversation with Martina's lie detector skills; she'd have to rely on steering the conversation in a different direction. "Maybe." Giselle sighed and dropped her head. "He was very interested in me. Made me uncomfortable."

Martina reached out and pulled Giselle into a hug. "You did come from their territory. That we know from your foster care records."

She stroked Giselle's hair lovingly, and despite her aversion to having this conversation, Giselle couldn't help but soak up the motherly attention. She listened to the slow steady rhythm of Martina's heart and relaxed into her arms, feeling almost childlike, remembering how much she had wanted this to happen when she was younger. Every family that had taken her in had held the promise of love and affection – something she desperately wanted – but none had kept their word. She'd have given anything for a mom to cuddle her and hum soft melodies in her ear when she was sad, or someone to climb into bed and snuggle with when the monsters came out at night. Childhood had been hard, filled with people who proved time and time again that she could not trust them. And now, sitting here in Martina's arms, she wanted to desperately to trust, but that part of her had been broken.

Martina sighed, letting out a hot breath that tickled the hair on Giselle's head. "I wish we knew more, but we weren't given the details of your birth and parents. I'm sorry."

Giselle reluctantly pulled away from Martina's embrace. "Long shot, really." She put on a brave face, but the tears were there, just below the surface.

"Honey, what did David say to you? The entire time you've been here, you've never seemed so bothered by it."

"He didn't say anything, really." Giselle shrugged. "Just asked me everything I know."

"And what do you know?" Martina's jaw tightened, and Giselle knew her fishing for more information had to be tied to the meeting she'd had earlier. Di and Taylor had already revealed that the witches had spotted her talking to Cassandra.

"That I have been bounced from home to home for as long as I can remember." Giselle's voice cracked with emotion. "That no one could ever love a freak like me.... until I was brought here." She took a steadying breath and let her words hang in the air for a moment. "Tell me about you and Gavin. How did you start taking in young wolves? How did you even know where to look?"

Martina pulled back, as if startled by Giselle's sudden change of subject. Long moments passed in silence before she summoned up a response. "Our friends the witches," Martina said.

"I should have guessed." Giselle faux-laughed and feigned an amused smile.

Martina's expression did not mirror Giselle's amusement. If anything, she seemed to appear more concerned by the conversation. "How are you and Damien doing?"

"Oh... We're fine."

"Good," Martina responded suspiciously. "Best to keep our friends close. Witches have long been our allies, here as well as in other places."

"And have relationships between wolves and witches lasted?" Giselle was taking a big risk asking this, knowing that if Cassandra's story were true, Martina would certainly catch on.

Her expression hardened. Giselle knew she'd struck a chord, and that confirmed that Cassandra had to at least in some small part have been telling the truth. But as soon as the expression flashed across Martina's face, it faded. "You mean, are you and Damien destined to be together forever? That's up to you two."

"But you've never seen it work?" She watched closely as Martina's eye darted away from her face. The slight kick to her heart was there too. Martina was definitely hiding information. How much of it was uncertain, but the claim Cassandra had to being her birth mother was still on the table.

Martina hesitated in answering. "It's not a relationship that's easy to maintain. We have different... agendas."

"Why can't it be maintained? What's wrong with it?"

"Nothing is wrong. Please don't think that."

Giselle could almost smell Martina's lie. "Damien said witches and wolves can't have kids or remain in a pack," she blurted out.

"He's right." Martina hesitated again. But though Giselle could tell she wasn't giving the whole truth, the small part she'd just revealed just blew Cassandra's story out of the water. "Damien is right, on both accounts. To remain together, you'd have to go it alone. But I don't see that being an issue for a very long time. You two are just kids right now. Enjoy being kids without worry."

"Right. Of course." Giselle let out a loud breath. "We're just kids. I'm being silly." She couldn't divulge what she'd learned now, nor tell Martina about what Cassandra has said.

Silence filled the room again. Giselle sat trying to process all she'd learned, but there were too many question marks. Every time she talked to someone, they revealed just as much truth as they disproved. Though one thing was becoming painfully true: both Damien and Martina agreed that children were not part of the equation. Surrogacy was a gray area, but there was a pretty decent chance that she was not Cassandra's kid, though the poor woman believed she was.

Martina finally broke the silence. "Please don't let our guests put too much worry into your mind. In another day they'll be gone, and you'll be back to normal life. The full moon is coming, and I think a pack run is in order for us all."

"That sounds great. I can't wait." Giselle stood and gave Martina a hug, glad for an out to this awkward conversation. She started to head upstairs. The girls would wonder what she'd said to Martina; if she'd mentioned the witch. She'd have to tell them something. Another lie. Something to appease them for the moment.

More and more, the reality of her destiny to be a lone wolf was rearing its head. Not fitting in anywhere, never knowing who to trust; these were the hallmarks of her life. If Cassandra was right – or, more worrisome, if what she'd heard about Cassandra was right – Giselle was the daughter or a criminal who'd used magic against wolves. That was no legacy to be proud of. Or on the other hand, if Cassandra had been lying, then she was being used for some unknown purpose and at risk for getting hit with the magical boom stick like that other poor wolf had. And she didn't want to end up like a hairy vegetable for the rest of her life. Wolves had long lifespans...

17

Funny how less than a week before, Giselle had been dreading the start of the new term, knowing that it would be oppressive and grueling, especially with her arch nemesis Mr. Harper; and yet now she craved the sanctuary of school. Freedom from supernatural bullshit. Teenage problems barely even registered on her crap-o-meter these days. The school day had passed uneventfully and surprisingly quickly, leaving Giselle sitting on the bench in the quad, knowing she needed to leave and go home, but desperately hoping for a reason not to.

Watching the other kids milling around the halls, stressing over what to wear and if the guy they were crushing on would ask them out, turned Giselle into a green-eyed monster.

Lucky bitches don't even know how easy they had it in life.

Teenage drama paled in comparison to what she had to deal with. Even boy troubles in her realm were steeped in supernatural bullshit. Normal girls fought with their guy over inattention or acting like an idiot, not because they were busted keeping magical contracts with her sister a secret. Regular girls never had to help to cool the tensions between warring packs ready to rip each other to shreds.

No. Normal teens worried if their eyeliner got smudged or if maybe their panty line was showing. Giselle's worries included sprouting a full-on fur coat and a set of canines that could rival Count Dracula's. And oh god, if that ever happened in public, a whole shitstorm would descend on her because her kind was supposed to be a secret. And while her kind were being all secretive, they'd excluded her in the process, and then got mad at her for doing the same. *Stupid double standards.*

Giselle caught the eye of a freshman girl, struggling to balance her purse, phone, and folders. She seemed so small and innocent despite the heavy layers of makeup and perfume that burned Giselle's nose from twenty feet away.

That girl's biggest worry this morning was whether or not her skirt looked good with knee-high boots. Which Giselle had to admit, worked really well! Even Taylor would approve of that wardrobe choice.

On top of her well-put-together ensemble, that freshman had it easy. Meanwhile Giselle desperately wanted to bare her soul to someone about Cassandra but feared saying a word to anyone, even her sisters now, because of all the rumors and speculation. Di's revelation was the most concerning: her potential mother, a criminal to the very pack that she came from.

But could she even call Cassandra her potential mother? Both Damien and Martina had said it was impossible. And that just opened the door to a whole other confusing round of questions about why Cassandra had fixated on her if they were not related.

Her head was threatening to explode from the stress, and she was just about to take off to the cafeteria for some caffeine when Taylor appeared.

"Peace offering," she said with a steaming coffee in hand.

"We're not at war," Giselle said, confused but eager to accept the offer. "I thought we were all cool after last night."

"Preemptive peace offering, then," Taylor said, smiling so hard the corners of her mouth twitched.

"Where did you get coffee?" Giselle asked.

"Helps to be a teacher's aid. I have access to the lounge. Coffee all day long... any time you want." Taylor was channeling a used car salesman with that pitch, but the prospect of a fresh source of caffeine was not something to scoff at.

"What did you do?" Giselle held the cup, afraid if she took a sip she was accepting Taylor's apology without knowing if she truly wanted to.

"I know more about Cassandra," Taylor said, cringing as if she expected backlash.

"What exactly do you know about her? Di already said..."

"Don't. Please. I know you're hiding things from us, and I won't even pretend to know why, but you need to stop now. We're pack mates and sisters. We have to trust each other at some point, so this is me offering you a truce and a chance to clue me in on what you're going through, so I can be a sister and help you through it."

Taylor's sincerity touched Giselle on a level she'd not thought possible. Her sister looked as if she were both sad and scared at the same time in approaching Giselle about this. There was no judgment in her eyes at all, only concern. Guilt smacked Giselle hard in the face. She'd been a loner for so long. She'd never trusted because she'd never had a reason to. But she'd never considered that it went both ways. All this time when she'd been wondering if she'd ever find her place, she'd never given a thought that maybe she was feeling that way because she put herself on the outside. And here was Taylor, right in front of her, begging to be let inside Giselle's messed up world.

The weight of her guilt pushed Giselle back down on the bench she'd been sitting on. "Okay. But I don't want judgment because I'm not even sure what I believe or want to believe about everything I've heard."

"Go on, then." Taylor took a seat next to Giselle on the bench in the quad.

Giselle blew out a breath and steeled her nerves. No more secrets. She was going to lay it out on the line and hope this didn't blow up in her face. "Okay. Cassandra came to me with a story about how she had been in love with a wolf and wanted to start a family with him." Giselle watched Taylor's face closely, looking for any hint of judgment. When she saw none, she continued. "But because witches and wolves can't have kids for whatever reason, she had to use a surrogate. She acted as midwife and cared for the surrogate during the pregnancy, but when the time came for the baby to be born, the surrogate disappeared. She thinks I'm that baby."

Taylor's eyes grew as wide as saucers. "That was not what I was expecting you to say."

"You said you knew about Cassandra. What did you mean?" Giselle suddenly felt as if she'd been played.

"I knew she was interested in you. And from what Di said, she was responsible for making one wolf go mental. I thought she was trying to lure you into some kind of magical contract to save her skin. She's going to be taken in for questioning by David and his group. But I never thought she'd spin a story like that."

"So you don't think it's possible?" Giselle asked.

"I wouldn't know. But that is like soap opera level drama."

"Yeah. *As the Moon Turns*." Giselle laughed. "I guess it is. Problem is, I kind of want it to be true. The mother part, not the wolf going crazy part. I want to have a link to family."

"You do, silly. With us." Taylor nudged Giselle, nearly knocking the drink out of her hand.

"You know what I mean. Haven't you ever wondered where you came from?" Giselle asked.

"My parents were killed when I was little."

"Sorry. I didn't mean to bring up a painful memory," Giselle said.

"Nah. I get it. I have closure. You're still in limbo. But do you really want Cassandra's past linked to yours?"

"Not the dirty laundry. Hell, no! The thing is, I didn't know that part until last night. You guys have been keeping just as many secrets from me, and it's causing more drama."

Taylor sighed and looked down, fiddling with her hands in her lap. "Damien asked us to keep it quiet. We thought he was doing the right thing at the time."

Giselle grumbled, "He's on thin ice with me."

"I think we all know that... Damien included," Taylor said. "He promised he'd make it up to you later."

"I'm not even sure I should give him a later. Martina confirmed that witch and werewolf relationships don't last. Maybe it's best to cut things off before we get too serious anyway."

"Awww, Elle, don't say that. He's a good guy. He really means well." Taylor's eyes drooped like a puppy dog's.

"The fact is, he knew Cassandra was on to me, and rather than give me the whole truth, he decided secrets and deception was the way to go."

"Because he knew she was crafty. She could be spinning lies to lure you in," Taylor said.

"But why? What importance is a stray wolf in the grand scheme of things? If Cassandra is lying to lure me in, for what purpose? I'm just a kid."

"That's what we need to find out... as a team." Taylor eyed Giselle with that *Don't even think about arguing with me* expression. "You drank the coffee; that's a legally binding agreement to peace."

"No, it's not. But nice attempt."

"Elle." She almost snarled the name.

"Playing." Giselle held her hands up in surrender. "You and me... We got this."

"Di too. You really need to include her."

Giselle sighed. Di's heart was always in the right place, but her attitude was as abrasive as sandpaper, especially when a gentle touch was needed. "I guess."

"Don't look so pissed off about it. She wants to help too. She just has a different way of showing it," Taylor said.

"I know. I'm being stupid." Giselle chugged her last bit of coffee. "Let's do this. Go team She-Wolf."

"No more coffee for you," Taylor laughed.

"Coffee or death?"

"See? I like the goofy Giselle. Be her more often, okay?"

"Help me get to the bottom of all of this, and I promise I will."

"Deal." Taylor pulled Giselle up to standing and led her down the hallway towards the parking lot.

18

Giselle and Taylor had taken so long to leave that the parking lot had completely emptied. Only Di's and the teachers' cars remained.

Sitting in the driver's seat, applying her lipstick in the rear-view mirror, Di sat waiting.

Her expression reflected the opposite of Taylor's caring and concern. She wore her annoyance proudly, like the shade of burnt orange lipstick she'd just finished applying. "About damn time, Elle!" Di speared her with a fierce look that said she'd better have an explanation.

"Sorry. Had to stop by the lockers. Forgot my lit homework." Giselle shoved her way into the back seat and busied herself with papers in her folder.

"You know that's not what I'm talking about." Di hadn't stopped staring her down, and it was beginning to make her uncomfortable.

"Go Team She-Wolf," Giselle faux-cheered.

"Bitch." Di laughed, and though her expression suggested otherwise, she genuinely seemed amused.

Giselle filled her in while Taylor squeezed into the passenger seat and closed the door.

"She's not your mom, but there has to be a reason she's pretending to be. I just don't see the connection," Di said thoughtfully.

"Neither do I. I've been running it through my head all day. If it's impossible to have kids that way, then I belong to another woman, so what good would it do her to claim otherwise?" Even though there were no new answers, Giselle felt the weight of the world lifting from her shoulders being able to share her doubts and fears with her sisters.

Taylor had been writing in her notebook, drawing lines from one side to the other, randomly crossing out phrases. "What if she's not really a witch?"

"Damien thinks she is," Di said.

"Because she wears an amulet and dresses like one. I've never seen her do magic, though," Giselle responded.

"Tell me about her. You've been in close; what is she like?" Taylor asked, still scrawling gibberish into her notebook.

"You've seen her. She's got to be Martina's age. Like forty or fifty, I guess." Giselle shut her eyes and tried to picture the last time she'd met with Cassandra. "She's got this funny sort of smell, like she's trying to smell like one of us – but it's fake."

"Weird. So she's playing at being a wolf?"

"I guess." Giselle shrugged. "Maybe. It's like a perfume."

"So she likes the smell of wolves?"

"Maybe." Giselle struggled to think of why. Wet earth was not the most attractive of scents. And she often used more perfume and body spray that she needed to mask her own personal aroma.

"Can you tell me anything else?" Taylor asked.

"She's sad." That was the fact that had struck Giselle the hardest. Every time she met with Cassandra, there were tears. The woman was clearly depressed.

"I'd be sad too if I had wolves and witches out for my head," Di said flippantly.

"Hey!" Giselle snapped at Di.

"It's the truth."

"I'd be sad too if I was falsely accused." Giselle might not have completely bought Cassandra's story, but she wasn't about to let Di drag her name through the mud just yet.

Taylor set down her pen. "What we need to do is find a way to get more intel on this Cassandra lady."

"Someone has been reading way too many spy novels." Giselle took a peek at the notebook Taylor had been working in. Her notes looked like the documentation of a crime, with big question marks next to phrases like *Whose baby?*, *Father knew too much?* and *Magical whammy?* The last one had Giselle laughing from the back seat.

"Whatever. At least I'm offering up some suggestions." Taylor scratched her pen across the whole page and tossed it back in her backpack.

"The packs all had a meeting last night with the witches. And I remember Asher saying his family's one-on-one dinner with David was tonight. As long as that hasn't been canceled, then there's still time to learn more. What we need to do is make sure the Alphas will have their dinner tonight, and then we can set up a meeting with Cassandra."

"Whoa. You think that's wise to set up a one-on-one with her?" Di asked.

"Why not? It's not the first time I've spoken to her."

"What?" Di asked.

"Save the drama for later. We're on the same team now, remember?" Giselle's tone was warning enough.

Di's expression soured. "I don't like the idea of meeting this woman alone."

"We won't be alone. We'll be together." Giselle tried to sound all team spirit and gung ho. "We're stronger as a pack, remember?"

"She's got a point, Di," Taylor said.

"Should we call for backup? Let Damien know?" Di asked.

"No!" Giselle said, louder than she meant to. "He's got his own secrets to keep." She intended it to sound thoughtful, but realized it had come out bitchy. "I mean, the witches are already dealing with so much. I don't want to draw him across enemy lines."

"Stop while you're ahead," Taylor said. "There is no way you can say it without sounding bitchy. We won't call Damien."

"But I will check in with Ash," Giselle added. He was the one wolf she had trusted from the beginning. She could ask him anything and expect a straight answer. It only occurred to her seconds later that Taylor was giving her the stink eye. Her issue with Asher would have to be dealt with soon enough. Giselle nearly blurted out that she was not trying to steal Taylor's man, but in the spirit of camaraderie, she opted with explaining why she wanted to talk to him. "I need to get a feel on the mood of Ash's pack before we start."

"That one you can do alone." Now it was Taylor's turn to throw out the bitchy attitude.

"I won't be long, though. I promise." Giselle didn't have time to add more boy drama to the mix. "In and out, just a quick fact-finding mission... like in your books."

"Whatever," Taylor groaned. "How are we going to get away with another night missing dinner?"

That was a serious problem. Dinner was a Martina staple, and they had already missed one this week. But she couldn't face Martina or Gavin with all the question marks hanging in the air.

Di waved her hand flippantly. "I got that one covered. Giselle is doing extra credit for Harper, seeing as how she needs the brownie points. So she's going to be collecting samples tonight in the desert. For Harper. Martina will just have to feed us early or let us skip out, because you know we can't go out alone."

Crafty, and fairly plausible. Giselle nodded in approval, and watched Di send the text to their den mother.

"So then what do we do once we get out?" Taylor asked.

"Stay close and let me make introductions. If her story checks out, then we have nothing to worry about. And maybe Martina and Gavin will listen to us if we present the information together. Convince one Alpha at a time," Giselle said, feeling hopeful and excited that her sisters had her back.

"And if it goes wrong?" Di asked, throwing a bucket of cold water on her mood.

"We're stronger together. She's just one woman," Giselle replied.

"She's a witch," Taylor retorted.

"Spells take time to cast," Giselle said with a weak smile.

"And you know this how?" Taylor asked.

Giselle shrugged. "Lucky guess."

"I hope you're right." Di pulled the car out of the parking lot and headed home so they could all put in appearances before they ducked out of dinner.

19

Next time she needed to get out of something, Giselle was going to go straight to Di. Not only had Martina allowed them to skip dinner, she'd sent them off with a picnic to enjoy before they got to collecting samples.

She'd nearly uttered the words "This was too easy" before giving herself a mental kick in the ass to shut up and not tempt fate.

The girls all climbed into the car and set off down the road.

"How are you going to get Ash to talk?" Taylor asked, not bothering to hide her annoyance.

"Going to do what I always do – just talk." Giselle tapped out a quick message on her phone to get Ash's attention and then pocketed it. "Drop me off at the end of the street, and I'll walk up to his house."

"You don't want us with you?" Taylor sounded almost hurt.

"Not just yet. It's easier if we don't gang up on Ash. He's got enough on his plate with Daddy and the Alphas." Giselle laughed at the understatement. Mr. Thrace could make drill sergeants cry, and

David being the Grand High Poobah of Alphas meant the stress level would be turned up to eleven.

"So what do we do, just drive around the block until you call?" Di asked, her tone decidedly neutral in comparison to Taylor's.

"Yeah, that's probably best. I'll text as soon as I'm done." Giselle got out at the end of Ash's street. His house, though only a few blocks north, was worlds away from the standard cookie-cutter neighborhoods she lived in. Here there were not only gates to get into the neighborhood, but each small street held a unique mansion-like home further gated from its neighbor. *Trick or treating must have been horrible for Ash.* She amused herself with the thought as she walked the short distance to his driveway gate.

She sent another quick text to let him know she was there. The gate rolled to the side with a loud creak. Giselle walked up the long drive towards the mansion that was the home of Ash's family and pack.

Asher met her at the door, closing it quickly behind him as if he were escaping without notice. "I didn't find your tank top. Are you sure you left it in my truck?" he asked, sounding more confused than curious.

It was a cheap lie, but it had worked its purpose. Asher had come out alone just as she had hoped, without needing to deal with Mr. Thrace or the rest of his pack. Asher, Mr. Rules himself, was nothing compared to his brothers.

Giselle shrugged. "I thought I had worn it as an undershirt. But maybe I lost it in the wash. Thanks for looking, at least." She tried to sound sincere and wondered if Asher saw straight through her ruse.

His narrowed eyes said he wasn't buying it. "Did you honestly come all this way for a t-shirt?"

"Tank top." She flicked at his chest playfully. "And I've had it since I moved in. It was the first thing they bought me. You know – sentimental, and all that crap."

"I can see you're so broken up over it. I'm calling bullshit. Tell the truth. Why'd you drop by?"

"Has he been by your house?" Giselle asked, looking around the driveway to see if any new cars had parked. Ash's truck took up most of the view. He wasn't allowed to park in the garage; that place of honor was for daddy.

Asher leaned against the cool stone wall and looked down, meeting Giselle's eyes. "They all met yesterday, and I thought that would be it, but no." He sighed. "They're due here in a couple hours – Mr. Silverman and his boys."

"And I'll bet you're super excited to hang with them, right?" Giselle laughed, remembering how protective he'd gotten with them the day before.

"I have to be civil. Nothing more."

Giselle mocked him – "I have to be civil" – then stuck her tongue out.

He clearly hadn't got the joke. Ash's mouth formed a hard line. "Are we done here?"

"Stop it. If you can't take a joke, we can't be friends, okay?"

"You're not a guy. You don't understand."

"Don't even go there, because I can open up a whole world of womanly issues on your testosterone-fueled ass."

That got him to crack a smile. "Okay, yeah. Testosterone causes male stupidity, is that what you want me to say?"

"Yeah?"

"Well, I'm not going to say it." He stuck his tongue back at her.

It might not have reared its ugly head often, but Asher at least had a little sense of humor, unlike other members of his family.

Giselle laughed. "Male pride is only a close second to testosterone-induced stupidity."

"Whatever. I'll play nice because I have to," Asher said.

Giselle rolled her eyes at his obvious issues. Boys were dumb. Girls too, though. Taylor couldn't hear Ash's name without getting all grumpy. "I'll put it to you this way. Without those guys, you're in for one hell of a crappy evening."

"That I believe. Dad's already in a frenzy. You know how he gets. Everything must be perfect, or else the whole world goes to shit."

"Why's he so stressed about things? Didn't they have that meeting last night? Formalities are over with, right?"

"Nah, that was for some other issue. Tonight's our official inspection or whatever." Asher crossed his arms again and leaned back against the wall.

"Did he say anything about that meeting? Martina and Gavin won't say a word. It's all hush hush conspiracy crap. Even Damien is keeping quiet. To be honest, I'm getting sick of this whole bullshit with the secrets."

"Still? He tells you everything."

"No, he doesn't." Giselle looked away to hide her anger. She wasn't in the mood to drag those feelings out again.

"Damn. Still in the dog house, huh?"

"Whatever." Talking to Asher about boy trouble didn't feel right at all. She scrambled to drive the conversation back on topic. "Speaking of... how are you holding up?"

"I'm fine. My brothers are here too for the big meet and greet."

"So glad I'm not in your family," she laughed. All men. A house full of testosterone was not her idea of a good night.

Asher smiled in that casual cute guy way that even now, after knowing him for so long, made her feel giggly and silly. "Join the dark side. We have cake."

"That does sound good." Just hearing about it had her salivating with want. Especially if it was chocolate. With a layer of fudge in the center. Damn, his offer was tempting. Her stomach grumbled with hunger. Sandwiches and baby carrots were all she really had to look forward to, thanks to their little plan of missing dinner.

"Father ordered quite the catering menu. Might be worth a night of discomfort. Think of all that buttercream frosting."

"Um. Who stole Ash and replaced him with a pod person? Since when do you know what buttercream is?"

"Too much time spent with Taylor. Food. Fashion. Boy bands. That girl doesn't ever stop talking about them. Some of it sinks in." He laughed somewhat uncomfortably, perhaps realizing after he'd said it who he was talking to. Both he and

Taylor had been really tight-lipped since the end of summer.

"So is this a thing? You and her?" Giselle dared to ask.

He shook his head. "Nah. We're friends. She's my English lit tutor."

"Does she know this?"

"Yes. We both agreed before school started back up that we were no good like that. She's a little too high maintenance for me. And, in her words, I've still got a stick too far up my ass for her."

Giselle snorted. "Well, yeah... ya do." And then it all made sense – why Taylor seemed so bent out of shape about him but refused to admit why. She'd probably never been on the receiving end of a "Let's just be friends" conversation. Clearly Taylor had more invested in the relationship.

"What about you and Damien? Is he going to remain in the dog house forever?"

A knot formed in her stomach. She hesitated before answering.

"Sorry, we were on a roll. I'll shut up now," Asher said, thankfully taking the hint. His icy eyes darkened for a fraction of a second before he turned away from Giselle. Silence trapped them in an awkward moment before Giselle's phone beeped and saved her.

She looked down: a text from Di. "Crap. I'm needed back at the house. Pack meeting."

"Have fun. If you can escape, dinner is at eight. Remember the buttercream." Asher gave her a quick hug and let her go.

"Save me a slice?"

"Sure."

Giselle took off down the street, never more thankful for the opportunity to walk away from that awkward moment. Once she'd hear the slam of the door closing behind her, Giselle picked up her cell and phoned Di.

"Papa wolf is babysitting tonight. We're go for Operation Intel," she said, as she walked down the sidewalk, talking on her cell to Di.

"We're not seriously doing this code name shit, are we?" Di replied. She flicked her headlights on to draw Giselle's attention.

"Taylor said we had to lighten the mood." She stuck her tongue out at Di as she approached the car. Di's lip curled in response, clearly not feeling as playful as she should.

Giselle hopped into the car and took the passenger seat. Taylor had the seat behind.

"So what's our next move?" Taylor asked.

"I'm texting Cassandra now to meet in the park again." Giselle was already tapping the message into her phone.

"And what? You're going to meet her alone, and we come join you, or what?" Di asked.

"Yeah, basically. She won't want to see a pack waiting for her, will she? I'll send a text when it's time to come in."

"Okay. But if I don't see a text in a reasonable amount of time, I'm busting in anyway." Di drove the car down the street, heading for the park by school.

"Just play it cool. I want to get her to talk without feeling like she's cornered," Giselle said.

20

Night fell later in the summer, and even at the tail end of the season the streetlights had barely begun to come to life as they pulled up to the school parking lot, close enough that Di could be there in a moment's notice but far enough to not raise immediate suspicions.

Giselle got out and started to walk down the hill to the park, trying to think of all the things she needed to say and questions she wanted answers to before she brought her sisters into the conversation.

Cassandra hadn't even come into focus yet, but the chemically enhanced scent of wolf hit Giselle hard, teasing her, pretending to be something it wasn't, a testament to the woman who wore it.

Magic, remember to ask about the magic and the wolf. Giselle fought to stay focused as she approached. The smell screwed with her concentration, begging her to get to the root of that first. *And the surrogate. Find out how that worked.*

She followed the smell to the source to find Cassandra sitting on a swing, lazily drifting forward and back.

She hardly looked like a criminal on the run: clean clothes and her hair brushed and tamed into a smooth straight ponytail at the base of her neck. No nervous twitches or furtive glances cast over her shoulder. The more Giselle stared at the woman claiming to be her mother, the less she believed the story that she could have been involved in something so terrible.

Cassandra's head popped up as soon as she heard the crunch of Giselle's feet in the dirt, and her eyes found their target. Smiling as if she'd just been presented an award, she hopped down from the swing and came to greet Giselle. "I've been waiting for this."

"You know why I called you out here?" Giselle asked, slightly confused at the happy greeting. Surely the woman had to know she'd learned more about her situation.

"You've spoken to your friends and returned to me." Her overconfidence had her reaching out for a hug, but Giselle stepped back just out of reach.

"Sisters."

"Call them what you like. They are not blood," Cassandra said.

"You claim to be – but I'm still not convinced."

Her smile faltered and she lowered her hands to her side. "What lies have they told about me? Please. I've suffered so much for the past. It haunts me like a specter."

Either she was a damn good actress or she was telling some measure of truth. She radiated so much sadness that Giselle too felt sorrow for disappointing Cassandra. She nearly gave in and accepted the hug she'd refused moments earlier, but reason won over emotions. "I'd rather hear the truth from you before revealing any stories I may know."

"You see how smart you are? That quick wit. I could not be prouder of you," Cassandra said, chancing a glance at Giselle, tears already welling in the corners of her eye.

It took all Giselle had to keep her voice neutral and not betray her own faltering emotions. "No more flattery. The truth, or I walk away." This woman was nearly in tears every time she talked to her. How could someone endure so much sadness?

"I'm glad you said walk away rather than alerting your boyfriend, who has no doubt filled your head with lies about me. I'm not evil." Cassandra's tone soured. "I'm a woman who has lost everything, when all I wanted was love and a family."

"And what happened because of your desire to have love?" Giselle asked.

Cassandra wiped her tears with her sleeve. "I lost everything."

"The man you loved?"

"He's gone."

Giselle locked eyes on Cassandra. Tears or no, she needed the truth. Blunt, honest, truth. "Gone or dead?"

"To me, they are one and the same," Cassandra sobbed.

"So he's still alive?" Giselle needed to hear confirmation.

"Yes. But he's not living. He might as well have been put out of his misery," Cassandra said.

"Why then did you tell me he was killed in an Alpha battle?"

"Because I wanted you to think proudly of your father. It is not dishonorable to die in battle,"

Cassandra said. "Wolves revere their fallen warriors, and your father was more than a warrior in his prime."

Giselle struggled to find feelings for a man she did not know. The idea of him being a great warrior should have meant something to her as well, but neither registered an emotional response. Her only interest was the truth, and she tired of having to act as a reporter leading with the questions instead of just being given the whole story. "What else have you kept out of your original story?"

"The things I have kept silent about are painful. You live in a completely different world than I do. Here you have companionship with other packs, and even the local witches are your allies. When I was younger, my people were looked at as tools and a means to an end. I was okay with that. I knew my place. My coven was friendly and did what we could to appease the wolves. We had the royals of the Alpha pack in our back yard. It was frightening; one misstep could mean death. But even with that, love blossomed between me and your father. And when things went south, my life was put in jeopardy by the very people I called family."

More side story. More excuses for not giving the truth. Giselle's patience was running thin, and already she'd felt the buzz of her phone – meaning Di was ready to crash the party. "Look, I'm not trying to sound insensitive. I'm sure you've had your fair share of crap, but my life was no picnic either. I need to know the truth before I can consider any of what you say. Because I now have what I have always needed: family, friends, and most of all, a pack."

"I was wrong to seek you out. I should have left myself in the shadows. No doubt you have heard the wolves are after me, and your local coven is working with them. Do you know what they'll do if they find me?"

"You'll be put on trial, I'm sure." She might not have known her pack her entire life, but Martina was fair, and even the Thrace pack, with all their rules and regulations, appreciated the letter of the law: innocent until proven guilty, and all that. If Cassandra were truly innocent, she had nothing to fear.

"I'll be put to death."

Or maybe Giselle was wrong about the whole innocent until proven guilty bit. "Why?"

Cassandra sighed. Her eyes darted all over the place, avoiding Giselle's constant glare, as if she truly hated what she had to say. "Because I am responsible for what happened to my husband."

"You hit him with the magical whammy on purpose?"

"No. I would never. I didn't even know it happened until after..." She sobbed again, breaking down into tears and choking on her words. "It all happened... and I was chasing her... and then... nothing. I don't even have my own magic anymore."

"So if it's not your fault, why worry? You're innocent."

"You're new to pack law. Threaten an Alpha, and you must be prepared to die. Your father was an Alpha, and I am directly responsible for his current vegetative state. Not by choice. Not even by desire. But I am responsible, so I will die."

"Then why did you put yourself at risk?"

"Because I had to know you. I needed to see the beautiful woman you had become." Tears ran unchecked down her face. "You're the key to solving what happened all those years ago."

How could she not believe Cassandra's story now? The woman was in full mental breakdown in front of her.

Before she could say anything, the sound of screeching tires caught Giselle's attention. Cars, plural, were heading her way in a hurry. She jerked around, looking for Di's car, hoping the sound was just her overprotective sister cutting someone off on her way to save Giselle from certain doom. But Di's care was nowhere to be seen. She looked down at her phone to check the message she'd ignored.

Di: *We're busted. Sorry!*

What the hell was that supposed to mean? Had Di turned her in? Martina had sounded all too convinced they were heading out rock collecting in the desert. And then she remembered Damien's witchy spy network. Of course – someone would have been keeping tabs.

A truck pulled up, followed immediately by three more dark colored cars. No way she'd escape on foot. Giselle stood there watching, her heart hammering in her chest, anger bubbling within her. She was so close to learning more! On the damn precipice of understanding, and they had to ruin everything.

The look of horror on Cassandra's face confirmed what she'd already said: if they caught her, she was as good as dead. "You?" She barely got the accusatory word out before taking off in a full run.

Giselle screamed, "No!" behind her, both to refute her accusation and because she knew it was over. She'd never learn the truth. Giselle started to move, but the guys were already on Cassandra's tail. Ace and Jay caught her by the arms before she could even make it past the swing set.

Cassandra screamed and thrashed in their grip, but could do no more. She was no match, and seeing this further proved to Giselle that she had truly lost her magic. Anyone when threatened fights with all they have; witches had magic, and that was power. Cassandra had nothing but her voice and the insults she threw at them as they carried her off into David's car.

No. She couldn't let this happen. Summoning up the strength of her wolf, Giselle sprinted to the lead car. She screamed for them to wait, to listen to reason and give Cassandra a fair trial, but her pleas were ignored. She grabbed at David's arm, ripping the cufflink out of his shirt as she struggled to pull his hand off of Cassandra.

His grip was iron; she couldn't budge him, though she tried with all her might.

Behind her, someone grabbed hold of her shoulders and pulled her backwards. She heard her name being called, but in the scuffle she couldn't differentiate between Cassandra's cries and those of the one trying to pry her away.

"You can't do this. Stop," Giselle screamed, tears flooding her eyes. Desperation had her clawing at any bits of flesh near her in hopes she'd get someone to stop and listen.

Her voice held no weight, only blending in with the fearful begging of Cassandra.

"She knows what she has done, and now it is time for her to make amends," David said, finally acknowledging her coldly. "And if you understood the full story, you'd not be so quick to help her, little wolf." He shoved her away into the arms of Gavin who'd been struggling to get a grip on Giselle.

"Then tell me the story." Giselle continued to thrash, trying to free herself from Gavin's grip.

"When you are old enough," David said, as he ducked into his car and slammed the door behind him.

Giselle broke free from Gavin's arms again and threw herself at the side of David's car. "She's innocent until proven guilty. You can't do this. I'm her daughter... I'm her child... You can't!" She beat on the vehicle even as it sped away, and collapsed in the empty space left behind. "I need to know... mother." Tears poured down her face, but she didn't care.

This was how life worked. The minute hope entered your life, someone stole it away.

When Martina came to pick her up off the ground, she'd hoped to see some measure of compassion, but none shown in the angry wolf's eyes.

"You have to help her," Giselle sobbed. "She's innocent."

"No. We do not." Martina, with the help of Gavin, hauled Giselle up off the ground and shoved her roughly into their car.

Never before had Giselle seen this side of Martina. But she had seen that look of disappointment on many a foster mother's face. She was a good as gone. And that was fine with her, if they allowed Cassandra to be killed before she could learn the truth.

"Listen to me. We have to go back. We have to stop this." Giselle struggled to reach the handle on the car door.

"She manipulated you." Martina's words were delivered like a sucker punch, though she looked much calmer than she'd been moments earlier.

"Where are Di and Taylor?" Giselle screamed. "They know—"

"They are back home, safe," Martina barked at her.

"They set me up." Giselle growled the words while vowing to never trust anyone again.

"No, dear. Damien warned us you were being set up. He told us she claimed to be your mother. Did you really think I bought your special assignment lie?"

"That jerk and I are finished," Giselle swore.

"You should thank him. He did the right thing. She's dangerous," Martina said. "She could have hurt you."

"No. She's the victim. She told me—"

"How she cursed David's brother?" Martina eyed her angrily through the rear view mirror as Gavin scooted into the driver seat and started the car. "Did you know he can barely function? He has to be spoon fed and wear diapers for the rest of his existence."

Giselle tried to picture it and summon up the appropriate feelings of sorrow for that man's plight, but he was a stranger. Intangible. Cassandra had been so close; someone she might have been able to save, if only she'd been allowed to tell her story. "What happened to that man wasn't Cassandra's doing."

"That's what she wants you to believe." Martina's voice matched the coldness of her eyes. "All magic comes at a price. And she made him pay dearly."

"For what?" Giselle grumbled, knowing the conversation was going nowhere. Martina had shut down all empathy regarding that woman and sounded dangerously close to doing the same for Giselle.

"A child," Martina snarled.

"She was in love. She wanted to give him a child."

"Witches and wolves cannot have children, dear. It's in our genetics. We don't match up. She couldn't give him a child. Only another wolf could, and when she did, Cassandra took her revenge on them both." Martina's words were ice cold.

"I don't believe it." Giselle grumbled and crossed her arms. Martina of all people should have sympathy – being unable to have kids had to have left a mark on her. Cassandra, in the short time she'd seen the woman, had shown all kinds of emotional scarring over this issue. That fact more than anything else made Giselle believe. Maybe not in the whole wolf-witch baby part, but that Cassandra had paid the ultimate price for something, and that something was completely unintended. And now they wanted her to pay an even higher price because she was the only one they could blame.

"You will forget this nonsense." Martina delivered her order with all the power of her Alpha behind it, and Giselle felt the compulsion to fall in line. "You will remain home for the rest of the Alphas' visit. Step one toe out of our house, and you won't have me to deal with – it will be David who issues punishment. Have I made myself clear?"

Giselle turned to look out the window, not wanting to meet Martina's eyes. The pull of her Alpha mother was strong. She couldn't deny the need to agree, but she fought saying the words.

"Answer. Now, Giselle!" Martina had never sounded so mad.

"I have no choice," Giselle answered reluctantly, though already trying to find ways around Martina's direct order.

21

Giselle stormed up the stairs, nearly tearing off the door to her room as she burst in.

Di and Taylor looked as if they were about to go before the firing squad. Both of them had been sitting, huddled together on Taylor's bunk.

"Before you say anything," Taylor started to say.

"Who told her?" Giselle demanded, anger giving her voice more sharpness than she had intended. She wasn't angry at them. They couldn't have betrayed her. That much she knew.

"The witches had her under surveillance. The minute we dropped you off, Damien texted that we were in trouble," Taylor said.

"I tried to text you," Di added.

"And what punishment did you get?" Giselle asked.

"We're all grounded until further notice." Di said. "No unsupervised runs. No dates. No missing dinner, that's for sure."

"Oh, man... end of the world there." Giselle's tone was all bitch.

"Look, we tried," Di said.

Frustration and feeling like her hands were tied behind her back had her snapping at her sisters when she knew better. "And we failed. And now they have Cassandra."

"What will they do to her?" Taylor asked, sounding as if she truly cared about this woman's plight. That at least helped to temper Giselle's bad mood.

Giselle let out a breath. "She thinks execution."

"Did you find out anything new?" Taylor asked.

"Not enough to paint a clear picture of what happened." Giselle shook her head, shoulders slumping in defeat. "I just don't get it."

"What?" Di asked.

"Why..." Giselle started to say but her train of thought derailed before leaving the station. Wolves and witches were supposed to be friendly. Cassandra said they weren't. But Martina said they were allies. *Cassandra thinks that she is or was a mom, but everyone else says it's not possible. Magic is supposed to make almost anything possible, but Cassandra has none. Why? Where did her magic go and why did it go?* There were so many blank spots in both sides of the story; the simple thing would be laying it all out on the line, but no one seemed to want to do that. Worse yet, Giselle was supposed to be a key to all of it, but she couldn't see how she could possibly fit.

"Um... Earth to Giselle." Di snapped her fingers in Giselle's face. "You with us?"

"Yeah, sorry. Nothing makes sense." On top of all the confusion, her head ached from all the crying she'd done. "It's just... Gah... Adults are so stupid."

Di snorted. "And you're the poster child for intelligence?"

"No. But one thing adults excel in is pig-headedness. It's their way or the highway. Like Martina telling me under no certain terms am I allowed to leave this house while the Alphas are here. Why can't I be involved in the trial? What reason do they have for keeping information from me that pertains to me?"

Taylor shrugged. "They're just trying to protect you?"

"From what?" Giselle asked.

"Getting hurt... I guess." Taylor said.

"Um... do you see the smeared mascara? Not doing a great job of protecting my precious little emotions, are they? So what is it? That maybe there is some truth and the Grand High Poohbahs of the wolf and witch world don't want to admit to."

"They have to uphold truth and the law," Taylor said.

"In public view," Giselle countered.

"Now who's the one with all the conspiracy theories?" Taylor laughed. "Don't pick on me for reading spy novels anymore."

"Laugh all you want. This whole thing stinks of a cover-up of some kind. Face it. If I could only figure out what the angle was." Giselle threw herself on her bed and stared up at the top bunk.

The room remained silent, none of the girls having anything more to say, leaving an ominous air that thickened the tension with each moment that passed.

Somewhere out in the hallway, Giselle overheard Martina say, "The decision will be made tonight."

Giselle's heart nearly stopped. No. She had to do something. Find some way to intervene. She was on her feet sprinting to the door in seconds, shouting,

"Please. You have to listen to me," as she barreled down the hallway toward Martina and Gavin.

The anger in Martina's eyes had not cooled since their car ride, and even now Giselle could see the smoldering rage within them. "No. You've caused enough trouble and clearly cannot be trusted to do as you are told. We are dealing with Cassandra, and you will remain here."

"You can't make me," Giselle argued, but she knew very well that Martina could.

"As your Alpha, I order you. Defy me, and there will be grave consequences."

Giselle huffed. "Toss me back into the system. I don't care."

Martina's eyes narrowed, and she took a step closer to Giselle, invading her personal space. She'd been intimidating before, but now Martina had turned positively frightening. "There are other ways to break a defiant pup. You will do as I say. Or I'll turn you over to David for punishment."

Could she do that? Giselle went speechless. She looked to Gavin for support but found the same anger there behind his eyes. He could normally be counted on to provide balance and calm, but now even he had joint a unified front to ban Giselle from trying to do what she felt was right.

"I don't want to be your enemy, Giselle," Martina said. "But you are leaving me with no choice."

Fear nearly held her tongue, but the sense that she could make a difference in Cassandra's fate gave her enough strength to respond. "Please! You're not listening. Cassandra is not as bad as you think she is."

Martina closed her eyes and took a breath. At least she hadn't outright bitten Giselle's head off for backtalk. That had to be a good sign.

"Giselle." Martina's sounded as though she were fighting to keep a civil tone. "You've known her all of a week, and you're blinded by this fantasy she's fed you about family. We are your family, right here. We care for you."

"I may not know her well, but I know people. I've met my fair share of them, good and bad, and Cassandra is not bad. She couldn't have done whatever it is you think she's done." Beating her head into a wall would be more productive. Even as Giselle pleaded, she found her words dying in the air.

"Honey, she attacked David's brother with magic." Martina would not be swayed, though she pretended to care, softening her tone again as she responded. "She's permanently damaged someone. That's not something good people do."

"You don't have the whole story. Something is missing. Just let me come with you. Let me talk to her."

"You've done enough talking." Martina's tone turned cold again. Any hope Giselle had of convincing her left. "You know, if you had come to me first, maybe explained about her and what she'd told you..."

"You'd have done the same thing you're doing now," Giselle threw at her angrily. "You expect me to trust you, but you won't do the same for me."

"The difference between you and me, young lady, is that I have not been sneaking around and lying about knowing this woman. You ask for trust yet you gave me none to begin with. This conversation is over." Martina turned and left Giselle standing there with Gavin.

"Can't you do something?" Giselle asked. "Please."

Gavin shook his head. "Sometimes you have to be the one to do the right thing first."

"Okay, yeah, I know I screwed up. But why let someone else suffer for my mistake?"

"You think she will suffer because of you?" Gavin asked.

"I don't think she's going to get a fair shake. She approached me for a reason. Maybe there's some truth to what she says. Might not be the whole truth, but some nugget of it is there."

The anger in his expression had faded, replaced by genuine curiosity. "Why are you so certain?"

"Just a feeling I got. The last time I chatted with her, I was watching how sad she was. We were at the park, and she was nearly in tears watching the kids."

"And that makes you think she's your mother?"

"No. Honestly from what everyone else has said, I know she can't be my mother." Giselle let out a deep breath. That fantasy had died earlier in the evening. "But that doesn't mean she hasn't felt the loss of a child. There's more to this story. I just know it."

Gavin put a hand on her shoulder. "Your heart is in the right place. Your head… that's somewhere else entirely. Just cool your heels here like Martina asked. Cassandra will be allowed to speak her truth to the council before anything happens. If there is any truth to save her, she has to be the one to bring it forth. Not you."

"But—" Giselle threw up her hands in frustration when Gavin cut her off.

"That's the best I can offer you. Now, back to your room. Study, listen to music, do whatever you have to do to take your mind off of this, because it is now out of your hands."

She'd go back to her room, as ordered, but she wouldn't lose herself in music. She had to figure out another way. The truth – all of it – would come out tonight.

22

Mind racing, frantically searching for a solution, Giselle walked on auto-pilot back into her room, barely registering that Di and Taylor were standing next to the wall, ears still pressed against it.

She breezed past them and went to sit on her bed.

"We heard," Di said with a forlorn tone that surprised Giselle. "For what it's worth, I think they are being a little too harsh."

"Understatement of the century there," Giselle mumbled.

"Sometimes the whole Alpha thing is overrated." Taylor took a seat next to Giselle, throwing an arm around her in a side-hug. "You know. 'Do as I say, not as I do' can be pretty crappy."

"Alpha means nothing to me. It's just a title," Giselle said in an angry whisper. "Good leaders should listen to their people."

"Martina is scared. I can hear it. If the big Alpha weren't in town, I'd bet she'd listen," Di said. "But you know how that works. She has to do what she is told, too." Di took a seat at the desk and picked up a magazine. She flipped pages like someone needing a distraction but not finding anything worth her time.

"Easy excuse for her, sending someone to their death." Giselle shrugged out from under Taylor's arm and stood. "Just following orders."

"Don't be so hard on her. It's not like they're just executing Cassandra; they said a decision was being made, so there has to be some kind of council making this decision." Di tossed her magazine aside and picked up her phone.

"Text Damien for me," Giselle said.

Di rolled her eyes. "Why don't you do it?"

"Because you're his lifeline right now. Tell him he needs to come talk me down." She hadn't quite formulated what she'd say to him when he arrived, but whatever it was, it would need to happen in a face-to-face conversation. She needed to hear the beat of his heart, smell the sweat on his pores. Learn how much of what he'd done was honest and good-natured.

"And what are we supposed to do while you have this little talk?" Di tapped in the message on her phone.

"Stay out of the way," Taylor snorted.

"You two need to talk with Ash and see what info you can get from him," Giselle said.

"Ash is your department," Taylor grumbled.

"You want to do this right now?" Giselle asked. With all the bullshit she was dealing with at the moment, Taylor's anger at being rejected by Asher was the least of their worries. And she was done walking on eggshells with her sister over it.

"Do what?" Taylor asked.

"Your whole beef with me and Ash. What's the deal?"

"Nothing." Taylor shook her head and looked away.

"Clearly something. You're pissed he doesn't want to be more than friends. I get that. But me and Ash are friends. We have been since I came to live here. I'm not trying to steal something from you. I'm just doing what I have always done. Is that so bad?"

"Look." Taylor sighed. "It's fine. You get what you want. He's not mine anyway."

"That's not what I want at all. I'm trying to be a good sister here. Asher is off limits as far as I'm concerned because you have an interest in him."

"But it's not mutual, so it's whatever..." Taylor said.

"Then don't give me crap for being a friend. That's all we are, okay?"

Taylor's angry eyes said she wasn't convinced. "I'm not going to say it's easy seeing you all flirty and laughing with him, if that's what you think."

"I'm his *friend*. Someone needs to take him down a notch or two, he's got an ego the size of California." Taylor laughed, and Giselle knew she had gained some ground on the argument. "I mean really, you've said it yourself – he's an ass. It's good to have someone around who can call him that to his face."

"He is an ass," Taylor agreed.

"Do you blame him, though? Look at his family. They demand perfection," Di said. "Oh, and Damien is on his way over." She held up her phone.

A knot formed in Giselle's stomach. Part of her really did not want to have this conversation, but a much bigger part needed to. Face to face.

"You going to be okay?" Di asked.

"Yeah. This won't be good," Giselle said with a heavy sigh.

Di stood, looking ready for a fight. "We got your back, you know."

"I know you do, but he's my boyfriend, so it's me who needs to have the talk. You guys have a much more important task: learning what you can about where they have Cassandra and when they're going to carry out any sentencing."

Taylor stood, gave a further sigh of sister solidarity, and nodded.

"Are we good, then?" Giselle asked Taylor.

"You promise you guys are just friends?" Taylor's voice carried more than just a hint of worry.

"We are just friends," Giselle confirmed.

Whether Taylor accepted that or not, Giselle couldn't quite tell, but at least she'd laid it on the line for her sister. No more walking on eggshells. More important things needed to be taken care of.

The doorbell rang downstairs, and the girls took a collective breath as if steadying themselves for the unknown.

"Do me a favor," Giselle said. "Send him up here to talk. Alone."

Di nodded and grabbed hold of Taylor's hand, pulling her from the room.

23

No matter how short a time, waiting sucked. Nerves clouded her mind, preventing Giselle from focusing on exactly what she wanted to say to Damien when he walked in.

So much anger. So much confusion. He'd lied to her; he'd gone behind her back; he'd spied on her. All of these were relationship-ending offenses in her book. And then there was the huge elephant in the room: confirmation that witch and werewolf relationships were doomed to fail anyway.

His clunky footsteps on the stairs preceded his entrance into the room, and for a moment, her heart skipped a beat when he opened the door and met her with his boyish smile.

"Thanks for calling me over. I was afraid—"

"Stop it." Giselle cut him off. "You don't get to speak first."

Damien's smile faltered. His Adam's apple bounced nervously as he gulped back whatever words he might have said next. His charms and sly wit were not going to be allowed the first move in this fight.

He'd hurt her more than she could find the words to say at that moment. She'd thought seeing him might change her mind, but his face, his expression – there was no remorse there. He'd walked through the door smiling as if they were a happy couple getting ready for a date. Where were the sorrowful eyes? Did he think he had no crime to be forgiven of? The more time she spent staring at him, the more anger welled within her, steeling her courage to do what she knew was best.

Giselle took a breath to steady her voice. "You know, maybe we should just call things off."

Damien's shoulders slumped "Please. Don't say that. I was just—"

"I don't want to hear any more excuses. The fact is, you and I, we're too different. Our families are too different, and no matter what either of us think, we're bound to our packs."

"It's not always like this." Damien's voice betrayed his emotions. There was the sorrow she'd needed to hear right off the bat. Only it was too late now.

"No. It's only like this when it matters." Giselle threw his words back at him.

"How could I know what would happen? You can't blame me for—"

"Not trusting me to seek the truth?" Giselle cut him off again. "Not protecting someone who might be innocent? You didn't even take the time to listen when I was trying to tell you what I knew. You believed your coven blindly and let them take that poor woman off to slaughter."

"That's not what's happening." Damien's pleading tone held no ground against Giselle's anger.

"Oh, because now you know what's going on? They blame her for David's brother going loony. He's the Regional-fucking-Alpha. You don't screw with the Alpha and get away with it."

"She's a witch," Damien yelled, and then immediately corrected his tone. "It will be up to my people to handle her."

Giselle scoffed. "Same difference. She's dead. Game over. The Alpha gets what the Alpha wants."

"Not if she can show proof to the coven that she did no wrong." Damien took a slow step toward Giselle. He met her the rage in her eyes and hesitated in reaching out to her, though his hand twitched with the intended motion. "My people protect their own."

"And how is she supposed to do that?" Giselle turned her head, not wanting to keep eye contact with him. Sadness, regret, longing: it was all there in the depths of his soul. But she couldn't bring herself to see past the actions that had led them to this point. Not now with Cassandra's life hanging in the balance. "She's not getting a trial."

"She's being brought before the coven... and the Alphas. There will be a trial."

"Not a fair one. If the Alphas demand it, your witches won't protect her," Giselle scoffed. "One woman isn't worth bad blood between them. This is personal for the Alpha David. His brother is the one that she's accused of injuring."

"I didn't know it was his brother," Damien said.

He spoke the truth; she could see it in his face. "If you'd talked to me instead of assuming I was causing trouble, I could have clued you in. I've been piecing the puzzle together all week without your help."

"I know I was wrong. Mother had me sworn to secrecy while this was being handled. The two guys they brought in earlier this week confirmed who she was," Damien said.

"What two guys?" Giselle asked.

"That first day at Sammy's – she had two guys with her at the table. They were paid to keep an eye out for her."

"Like bodyguards?"

"Yeah, I guess."

"So, humans?"

"Yep. Mom had to wipe their memory before sending them on their way, and once they were gone, we were set to bring her in, but the wolves intervened."

"Because of you – talking to Martina. If she hadn't followed up on Di's lie about the science extra credit project, I would have learned all I needed from Cassandra."

"I know it all went to shit. It wasn't supposed to go this way. I fucked up. I'm so sorry!" His voice echoed the emotion of those words, but it wasn't enough for Giselle. Words were too late now. The only thing that could fix any of this was action.

"So then grow a pair, and help me prove her innocence. And then your coven can do their job and protect their own."

"You know I have no power when it comes to the coven. I'm just a kid."

"And that's exactly why this" – Giselle pointed to him and then herself – "is not going to work in the long run."

Damien threw up his hands in frustration. "You're blaming me for being a witch."

"No. I'm blaming you for not having the guts to stand up and do something. Your duty to your family is what's important here, not finding the truth."

"And you can't tell me your duty is any different?" He threw the words back at her.

"I can. Because I am an individual first and a wolf second." Anger had her teetering on the edge of shifting and letting her wolf finish the argument. But she held tightly to her self-control. "Yeah, my family will be pissed at me. Maybe they'll send me back into the system again, but I'll be damned if some woman dies because I didn't do all I could to prevent it."

"And if you're wrong about Cassandra?"

"Then I'm wrong, but at least I'll have tried to do the right thing."

"And how will you prove she's telling the truth about anything?"

"I don't know." That was a question she had not come up with an answer to. Giselle turned around and let out a calming breath. She needed a clear head to think. All the information was there. She'd gleaned so much from everyone she'd spoken to, but putting the facts in order left her with a headache. So many things seemed to fit, but nothing in the right order – like assembling a puzzle without seeing the image of what it should look like in the end. Cassandra was a witch. That much was certain. But one with no power. Why? Her gaze fell to the computer desk just for something to look at while she collected her thoughts. Di's magazine was there, with a gorgeous model on the cover wearing some feathered monstrosity that was supposed to be a dress. And the answer hit her just like that. Di had a secret she couldn't tell because of … "Witchy mumbo-jumbo."

"What?" Damien asked.

Giselle spun around on her heel, pointing a finger at Damien's chest. "Your spells are a magically binding contract, right?"

"Sure." he shrugged. "What are you getting at?"

"Cassandra might not be my mother. She might not have any relation to me what so ever. But, she used magic to help me come into this world."

"Okay." Damien's eyebrows quirked up, with curiosity more than confusion. "Go on."

"And what happens when someone spills the beans about magic that's been used?"

"There's usually a backfire of some kind. Something that negates the magic used for both parties."

"Well, what if I was already born, and someone spilled the beans, outing both Cassandra and the wolf? The backfire would have to come in some other form, right?"

Damien nodded slowly. "Sounds possible."

"So good old Dad lost his marbles. And Mom…." Giselle said hoping he would catch on, but he still looked to be one stop short of her train of thought.

Damien shrugged.

"She's dead, according to Cassandra. A life for a life."

A flicker of understanding glinted in Damien's eyes, but even now with her spelling it all out for him, he didn't seem completely convinced.

Giselle let out an exasperated breath. "Have you ever seen Cassandra use magic?"

"No."

"Maybe because she lost hers."

"Oh, right." His eyes widened with realization. "But who told? What caused the backfire?"

"The other woman! You know... Mom. The real one."

"So the lady who thought her baby was being taken away spills the beans and causes the backfire. But why then did you end up in foster care?"

"Because she's dead," Giselle said.

"So the only other person involved in this mess is dead. You're not going to convince anyone of Cassandra's innocence without some kind of proof."

"I'm the proof. I'm here. Alive and well, right?"

"How are you proof?"

"They can test my blood. If I match the Alpha's brother, then I was the baby in question," Giselle said.

"How does that clear Cassandra's name?"

"Cassandra thinks I'm her kid. But why? Witch and wolf don't mix. I highly doubt magic can help it along either. I'll bet that Cassandra *thought* I was hers because the surrogate kept secret that she was truly pregnant with the Alpha's baby. That didn't stop her from using nine months' worth of magic to ensure the pregnancy went off without a hitch. When it came time for me to be born, there was no going back. The surrogate, my real mom, took off. She must have told someone about what was happening to safeguard her and the baby – me – but then it all backfired on everyone. Dad, Mom, and witchy lady all got hit with the magical boom stick, and I was left alone in the world."

"That's a crazy story. You should write a book. Seriously."

"You don't believe it?" Giselle threw her hands up and growled in frustration.

"I don't know what to think." Damien took a cautious step backwards. "A good story doesn't clear Cassandra."

How can he be so thick? It all made perfect sense to her, but if Damien wasn't getting it, the rest of the council that was set to condemn Cassandra wouldn't either.

"Why would Cassandra risk getting hit with the magical whammy herself?" she asked.

Damien looked thoughtful for a moment and then shrugged. "No witch wants that."

Finally. She was dragging Damien down the path of understanding. "Right. She lost her magic in the deal. No witch willingly does that."

"But it has happened on occasion," Damien said with a sigh.

"Not of the witch's choosing, though, right?"

Damien shook his head. "Not if they can help it."

Baby steps. "So. If anything, she should have sought revenge for what had been done, because whoever broke the magical contract caused her loss of magic."

"Yeah. Right. If it were me. I'd be pretty pissed, sure."

Giselle hoped he was catching on. "But there was no one for her to seek revenge on. So she's been living as a magic-less spinster for all this time, trying to track me down, the baby she helped create. We need to make her prove she has no more magic, because that's proof that she was innocent in this. Because like you said, no one willingly does this to themselves."

Damien nodded for a moment then stopped. His brow furrowed. Giselle watched the wheels turning, hoping that he had truly put the pieces together as she had.

"Here's what I don't get." Damien said. "Why be silent all this time?"

"Because she had no proof of the event. She was in love, and because of her relationship, she was asked to leave the coven and her husband left his pack. They were alone. No real witnesses. I'm sure by the time David found his brother, Cassandra was long gone and her coven had already disowned her. No witness; no innocence. Just her word against his. I am the proof of the event. If they hadn't all gotten into bed together on this magical plan, I wouldn't be here. Without me, it's all hearsay. And we know how tight-lipped you witches are about magic, so with no one to vouch for her, how was she supposed to prove her innocence? You see, I am the key." Cassandra's words came back to haunt her. She really was the key to all of this.

Damien nodded and headed for the door. "Then we better go tell someone."

"I've been ordered to stay put," Giselle said.

"Since when do you follow orders?" Damien asked.

"Since I don't know where they are holding this council."

"It's not at my house, I can tell you that. Mom was all too happy to hear I was coming to keep you company."

"I doubt it would be at any of our homes, as it seems all of our leaders are dead set on keeping us *kids* out of it." Giselle slumped down on the bed. She'd hoped Damien would know more, but even now, after all the secrets and lies, she could see he was telling the truth. And that sent her heart sinking in her chest. If they couldn't find her, the information they had would be of no use.

24

Sitting helpless in this silence only served to amplify Giselle's defeat. For all she knew, the deed had already been done and an innocent woman had gone to her grave.

Anxiety whispered negativity into her mind. She might have helped the situation by being more honest about Cassandra in the beginning. She too was just as guilty for letting the situation get so out of hand. She could have gone to Martina first and explained. Hell, she could have gone to Gavin. He had generally been the most laid back of the two. She could have told her sisters early on as well. Lone wolf instincts had ingrained themselves deep in her very soul, and she wondered if she'd ever feel truly capable of giving herself to a pack.

And then there was Damien. A witch.

Cute. Funny. Charming. He was a great catch, but if this situation had proved anything, it was that they were destined for failure. She stole quick glances at him while he busily texted on his phone. Frustration etched lines all over his face, giving age to his features that looked out of place.

In twenty years, would that be the way he looked? Would they still be close then? Friends or enemies?

Supernatural bullshit, she mumbled to herself.

"Giselle, get down here," Di called frantically from the bottom of the stairs. "Hurry! Our ride's here."

Giselle and Damien eyed each other curiously for a moment before she summoned her voice. "Do you know what she's talking about?"

Damien shrugged and pocketed his phone.

"We better get down there then." She was on her feet and at the door in seconds. As soon as she opened it, the smell of wolf told her exactly who had arrived to play taxi.

Below, in the living room, Asher was talking to Taylor in a whisper that Giselle couldn't quite make out. They looked civil, thankfully. Especially given the conversation she'd had with her sister earlier in the evening.

Di looked up impatiently at her and Damien. "Have you two made up yet? We have business, and I don't need some breakup or whatever making you two all cranky."

Giselle refused to answer; she planned to reserve judgment until after the Cassandra situation had been dealt with. Priorities. But not wanting to waste any time, she took the stairs at a run. Damien followed in her wake, remaining curiously silent. She'd left things just as ambiguous with him and wondered how that might affect the rest of the evening herself.

At the bottom of the stairs, Giselle headed straight for the door, ready to take off. "Do we know where we're going?"

Asher turned from Taylor, his expression grim. "I have an idea of where they might go to be alone for official pack business."

"What are we waiting for?" Giselle asked.

"You know my dad will throw me to the wolves for disobeying, right?" Asher asked.

He didn't want to go. That much she could tell, and she couldn't ask him or any of them to put their lives on the line for her or Cassandra. This was her fight, and she'd be damned if someone else got hurt in the crossfire.

"Yeah, Martina threatened the same to us." Giselle tried to act as if she were not frightened of the consequences, but the unknown had her swallowing down a hard lump of fear in her throat. "I'm the one that needs to handle business here."

"Is she really worth it?" Asher asked.

Giselle looked around the room at the worried expressions of her siblings and friends. "Look, tell me where to go. I'm doing this alone. That way no one but me gets into trouble."

"You wouldn't last a second walking in alone, Martina's kid or not. You were told not to go. Defying your Alpha caries a heavy punishment." Asher pulled his keys from his pocket and took a step toward the door.

"This is my fight." Giselle swiped the key from Ash's hand.

"No. That's not true." Asher took his key back and looked down on her, his face a mix of determination and disappointment, as if her trying to protect him from trouble went against their bond of friendship. "We're all in this. We're the future of our packs. We have just as much duty to see right done by our kind. If you believe this witch is being tried unfairly by the wolves, then I'll go and stand by your side."

"So will I," Damian said, pushing his way between her and Asher to take Giselle's side.

A moment of awkward tension rose up between the two males; not something any of them had time for or that would earn them any additional favor with Giselle. Cassandra was the priority now.

"We got your back too, but you already knew that. Bring on the worst!" Di said, thankfully interrupting the tense moment with her can-do attitude. She and Taylor pushed the boys aside and opened the front door. "You guys coming?"

25

The barren desert blurred into shapeless lumps as they drove down a long stretch of highway. Night here remained wild and untamed with hardly a streetlamp, leaving nothing to see or landmark to figure out where you were. Only the occasional mile marker sign indicated how far into the nothingness you'd driven. Blaring light from the halogen lamps on Ash's truck announced their approach to any who might call this desolate land home.

Giselle had lost track of where they were. With the eerie glow of the Las Vegas strip hidden behind the mountains, her inner compass spun round and round, leaving her completely at the mercy of Ash's navigation skills. If they somehow got separated, she'd never find her way back. No wonder he thought the meeting would be out here.

It wasn't until a large bonfire in the distance confirmed they were heading in the right direction that Giselle felt any sense of hope.

Even that was small, knowing she was heading into hell.

"So, we're just going to crash the party?" Asher asked.

"Unless you have a better idea," Giselle said.

"We talk to Mom," Damien said.

Giselle turned an angry eye on Damien. So much for keeping their actions under cover. "Really? You told her we were coming?"

"He might have done us a favor," Asher said, surprisingly coming to his aid. "If we crash the party, they'll treat us with equal disrespect. If we are brought in as witnesses, then they have to listen."

"Screw the politics," Giselle grumbled. Damien could have at the very least said what he was doing. Again with the secrets! Her decision about him was being forced the more this situation unfolded.

Damien at least had the courtesy to look ashamed this time. "Look, I had to. They'll have some kind of magical protection to keep outsiders from interrupting. And like Asher said, you want them to listen, right?"

Giselle covered Damien's mouth, not wanting to hear his voice any longer. "You don't get to speak."

Asher pulled up behind a group of cars. By the looks of it, everyone had been called into this high-profile case. The entire witch coven appeared to be in attendance. Martina and Gavin were here. And Mr. Thrace and his other boys were too.

David was there. In the distance, she saw him seated like a judge in a large camp chair with the twins, Ace and Jay, on either side of him.

She struggled to see if Cassandra was there, but with all the other cars in the way, she was hidden from view.

A woman wearing a long flowing dress walked their way, weaving through the parked cars. Her jewelry and bangles clanked and clattered as she moved, creating a certain cadence to her steps.

"Looks like Jasmine's coming." Giselle stepped out of the truck and led the group to meet Damien's mother. The High Priestess's expression mimicked the way Giselle felt: angry and resentful.

"Firstly, I do not approve of what you have done, or the trouble you've gotten my son into," Jasmine spoke through gritted teeth, casting her heated glare directly at Giselle.

She had no quarrel with Damien's mother. The whole politics of the supernatural world was where her problems lay, but she wouldn't be blamed for Damien's actions. He had free will and could screw up all on his own as he saw fit.

Giselle took a breath to help steady her voice. Knowing she had already been given the black mark, civility was what was needed here. "I'm here because I think you all have it wrong, and I don't want to see someone innocent get hurt. You of all people should appreciate that. I'm trying to help one of your own."

"Don't you dare take a disrespectful tone with me!"

Not even two steps closer to the bonfire, and it seemed Giselle's argument was falling on deaf ears. She gritted her teeth, hoping to restrain her annoyance. If Jasmine wanted disrespectful, she could hear what it truly sounded like. No; that wouldn't solve anything. But it would make Giselle feel so much better to unload on someone for all the crap they'd put her through. Another deep breath. If this was the way she would be received, there was no hope for Cassandra.

Calm. Breathe. Be nice.

"I'm trying. I really am," Giselle said.

Jasmine's lips pursed and she looked away, setting her next target on Damien. "You will have consequences coming here."

Damien nodded, dropping his head, and mumbled, "I know, Mom."

Taylor and Di came up on either side of Giselle and grabbed her hands. The show of solidarity was more than invigorating to her waning spirit.

"Give us a chance. We're good kids," Taylor said, with her easygoing tone partnered with the smile that had won a spot in the Homecoming Court last year.

Jasmine placed her hands on her hips, bangles and bracelets clinking together as they slid down her wrists. "You can bring forth testimony, and then you will leave. I can offer you no more."

Giselle opened her mouth to speak, but before any snarkiness could come out, Di clamped her hand over it.

"Good enough. Lead the way, please," Di said.

Asher and Damien took the rear as Jasmine lead their little group into the center of the council.

26

Seated next to the bonfire, close enough for the heat to become uncomfortable, was Cassandra. Gone were her pretty clothes; she'd been stripped down to a plain cloth dress. Arms and feet bound so she could not run, she'd been set on a small chair facing her three groups of condemners. Richard, David's enforcer, stood like a silent sentry next to the accused. His presence confirmed without words that he had one purpose here in these proceedings: executioner if a guilty verdict was delivered.

The bulk of his muscles showed, even under his dress shirt. He could probably snap her neck in a heartbeat, and she'd never feel it.

The horror of that image sent a nervous chill down Giselle's spine. She couldn't watch an execution, and sent up a silent prayer to any gods that might be willing to listen to spare this poor woman.

To her far left sat the council of witches. They mumbled amongst themselves as Jasmine brought Giselle and her group forward, directly in front of David and his boys.

"You!" David pointed a finger straight at Giselle. Flames reflected in his eyes, but she could see beyond the fire to the true anger within. She'd riled the Alpha of the Alphas, and she knew no matter how this ended, she'd pay for her actions. "Go back to your homes as your Alphas have demanded. You will be dealt with in due course."

Now or never. Giselle gulped back the knot of fear that had suddenly formed in her throat, stealing the conviction of her voice and turning it to a meek croak. "I can't... until" – she cleared her throat loudly and took a breath, calling up her wolf for additional strength. Even her inner beast feared the retribution of this Alpha, but she had to do this – "I have had a chance to speak." Giselle shouted, finding her voice a little late. From the corner of her eyes she saw horror and then disappointment flash across Martina's face. No escaping the world of trouble she'd be in later.

"You are not of age and cannot be included in these proceedings," David responded, mocking her with a self-important chuckle.

Giselle had no retort. She could do the petulant child thing and just shout, but she knew that wasn't going to get anyone to listen. If anything, it would only work against her, making the wolves ignore her words. She turned briefly to look back at her group for support or guidance.

Jasmine spoke up, calling the attention away from Giselle's silence. "This child is directly involved, I'm afraid, and as such has to be given consideration under our laws."

"Whose laws?" David demanded.

"Witch law, wolf. Remember that we share equal presence here at this council." Jasmine's sharp tone and aggressive stance toward David had Giselle's full attention. The witch had no fear as she spoke. And maybe Giselle shouldn't either. She had the protection of the witches right now as a witness.

One look at David, though, reminded her that she'd be dealing with him later without that protection, so she'd have to choose her words carefully. He already looked as if he were going to chew his own cheek off.

Giselle cringed at the sound of his teeth grinding as he sat considering Jasmine's words. She looked back at Cassandra and tried to get her attention, but the witch was off in another world. Drugged or under a spell of some kind, it was like she was there but not.

"Fine. Bring forth your evidence," David said reluctantly.

Giselle stepped forward and delivered her side of the story, piecing all the bits of the puzzle together as she had done for Damien. She'd expected they would see reason, but found only anger and hatred behind David's eyes.

"You came all this way to tell me that bit of fiction?" Clearly not convinced, David waved her off with hardly a flick of his wrists.

"Call it what you want, the facts add up," Giselle said.

"What facts?" David threw Giselle's words back in her face. "You have nothing but rumors and the word of a convicted witch about to be sentenced."

"Innocent until proven guilty," Giselle snapped at him.

"We may live in America, sweetheart, but *you* are under *my* laws. Now leave. You're already in enough trouble."

Giselle stood her ground. "No! You wake Cassandra up and ask her the truth."

A growl rumbled up David's chest. She caught the prickle of hairs on his arm and worried she'd riled him too far. A tough girl she might be, but even Giselle knew her limits, and taking on the Alpha of Alphas was not a fight she'd win. Still, she had to do whatever she could. She had to do what was right.

"This is your last warning, pup!" David spoke through gritted teeth. His wolf was so near the surface she could see his teeth elongating.

Still, she knew she was right, and backing down would only mean losing the fight for an innocent woman. Giselle stood her ground, crossing her arms as if to say she would not be moved.

With only a glance, David had instructed his boys to move. Quick as lightning, Ace and Jay were at her side, gripping her arms, and lifting her off the ground.

"Hey! Get off!" Strength of will did not equate to fighting strength, and Giselle knew she was not going to be able to take on both the Silverman boys.

"Let her go!" Asher yelled, and moved to block their path as they tried to take Giselle back to the parking area.

"This is not your fight," Nathaniel Thrace bellowed from his position in the Thrace pack, but he did not move out of ranks. "Stand down, Asher!"

Jay tried to push past Asher, but the wolf stood his ground, a wall of muscle with the glint of daring in his eyes. Damien joined him to block the brothers from taking Giselle away.

She beamed a genuine smile at Asher and Damien coming to her aid, and tried to use their blockade as a way to wriggle her way free from the brothers' grip, but they held her firm, keeping her feet from touching the ground so she could not gain traction.

"Do you always blindly follow orders?" Giselle asked in frustration.

"Part of the whole wolf gig, you know?" Ace whispered back, sounding as if he would rather not be doing this, but that did not matter.

Giselle turned to David. "You'd send your own niece away?" She hoped throwing the relationship angle at him might appeal to his sense of family and pack.

"That has not been proven," David responded coldly.

"Then take the time to prove it, because it means Cassandra is telling the truth," Giselle said. "And you wouldn't want to lose another family member, would you?"

"But you are not her daughter, and you freely admitted it. Your true mother had to have been the unfortunate victim of Cassandra's magic, and she was punished for that with the loss of her own," David said.

"Whether or not I am Cassandra's daughter remains to be seen, but either way the story unfolds, I am your brother's kid. You should take that into consideration."

"What I am here to pass judgment on is what happened to my brother, and Cassandra is directly responsible for that," David said. "Your relationship is only a secondary annoyance."

"Cassandra got hit with the magical whammy." Giselle threw back at David and then turned her gaze to Jasmine. "How does a witch lose her magic?"

Jasmine looked from Giselle to Cassandra and back again. "She may only lose it in breaking a magical contract."

"Can you not bind a witch's power?" David asked.

"You cannot take away that which is part of a person's soul. You can try to prevent its use, but no one can take a gift that is not theirs," Jasmine responded. She walked over to Cassandra, coming up nose to nose with her, ignoring the angry growl from Richard, and whispered a few words in prayer.

As If from a dream, Cassandra woke slowly; and then, upon realizing where she was, began to panic. She struggled and pulled against her restraints, moaning and crying out for mercy.

"Hush now, be calm and speak your truth," Jasmine said.

Cassandra's wide eyes narrowed on David. "You bastard!"

"Careful now, witch. You're on trial for your life." David smiled wickedly.

"I did nothing wrong," Cassandra pleaded.

"That is a lie, my dear." Jasmine spoke calmly, but underneath the civility there were distinct notes of anger. "Improper use of magic is clear, and will be dealt with in turn. You will need to be completely honest about the rest."

"Tell us about the baby," David asked.

"She's here." Cassandra's eyes landed on Giselle. Tears streamed down her cheeks. She dropped her head, sending her gaze to the ground as if to embarrassed to be seen as she admitted her past. "I used magic to join my body with a wolf from

Orion's pack. We were one woman, in body and spirit for the mating ceremony with Orion."

A collective gasp came from the witches nearby.

Cassandra took a sobbing breath and continued. "And then spent the next nine months watching over the she-wolf as her midwife."

"So you do not deny using forbidden magic to create a baby of both witch and wolf?" David asked, smiling as if he had already won.

"I do not," Cassandra said somberly. "But look at the results."

Giselle felt a sense of pride seeing how Cassandra spoke of her. She had been truly wanted. For a girl who'd spent her entire existence in the system, unwanted and alone, this meant the world to her. She'd needed to hear it more than anything else in her life. She was wanted. And that thought gave her strength to speak. "And that wolf double-crossed her and blew the magical secret when I was born, causing everyone involved to be hit with the magical boom stick. Cassandra's loss of magic is proof of that."

"She truly has no magic?" David said. "Sounds more like a magical backfire for attempting to create a hybrid abomination."

Giselle snarled at his insult to her. How dare he pretend to be a great leader and call her an abomination? But before she could find the words, Cassandra responded with her own anger.

"She is no more an abomination than you are, David! And my intent was to have a child to love and raise with my husband."

"Your intent cannot be proved or disproved," David said. "What has been proved is that my brother, Orion, was shortly thereafter rendered incapable of living a normal life. In my opinion, a good cover-up to ensure your improper magic stayed secret."

"I loved Orion. And I had every intention of loving my child too," Cassandra said. "I woke up to my husband incapacitated and my baby gone with that woman. I couldn't even perform a simple spell to locate her."

"Why did you not go to your coven for help?" David asked.

"You know as well as I do that I'd been banished from my coven when I took Orion as my husband," Cassandra said. "You banished your own brother for the same reason."

David's eye twitched and his confident smile faltered.

Giselle saw the predator in him, ready for the kill. He wouldn't let her off even if proof of her innocence was laid right in his lap. He wanted blood – revenge for his brother, no matter the cost.

"Don't you see?" Giselle interrupted their staring contest. "This isn't about justice at all. Both packs here have to see this. Martina, Nathaniel... er, Mr. Thrace... please. Here is a woman who screwed up a little and is about to be burned alive for a crime she didn't commit. Let the witches deal with her magical mess up, but don't let her life be taken in revenge. Can't you see she's lost everything already? She has no family, no husband, no kid." Giselle hoped her appeal wouldn't fall on deaf ears, but even within her own pack, Martina and Gavin wore expressions of disappointment rather than compassion.

Mr. Thrace looked as if he were ready to bite his own son's head off.

Di and Taylor stepped forward, each putting a hand on a brother's shoulder.

Ace and Jay softened their grips on Giselle but did not let go, still waiting for instructions from their leader.

27

Time stood still as everyone waited for something to happen. The bonfire had become a Mexican standoff with Giselle, Cassandra, Jasmine, and David all locked in a silent game of chicken, each person daring the other to say something or make a move. Aggression ran thick in the air as if at any moment they'd all erupt into their wolves and take to using brute strength to ensure their will was enforced. The air above crackled with magic. Jasmine might not have been wolf, but Giselle could bet she'd have some quick spells at the ready to defend herself if need be.

"Enough with this charade," David finally broke the silence. "We'll put it to a vote. On the charge of improper use of magic, raise your hands if Cassandra is guilty."

Unanimously the groups lifted their hands.

"Sentencing to be carried out by Jasmine and her coven," David said with a smile.

"On the charge of willful injury to an Alpha wolf, raise your hands if Cassandra is guilty," David said again.

When no one, not even Richard, raised his hand, the vein at David's temple became visible. He gnashed his teeth and a growl rumbled out behind them. "This woman left a once-proud member of our own disabled and helpless. Does this not mean anything? For seventeen years now, he has been sentenced to this half-life while she walks free. How is this justice?"

Martina stood. "It is justice because a price was paid by all parties. He went against magical laws and paid with his mind. Cassandra paid with her magic. And we can only assume the other wolf paid with her life. There is no debt of justice left to collect."

"No!" David was on his feet bearing down on Cassandra, a predator ready for the kill. He shifted mid sprint, tearing his clothes apart as the enormity of his wolf took form.

Massive and dark as night, the shape of David's wolf sent a fearful chill down Giselle's spine. She jerked in Ace's and Jay's grips as he brushed past her on his way to Cassandra.

Richard, the silent and unmoving sentry, locked eyes with David. His movements, cloaked in a blur of fur and fire and amplified by the terror-filled shrieks of Cassandra, made Giselle fear for the worst. But as the dust settled, Cassandra appeared unharmed.

Richard in mid-shift, standing on human legs and partly covered in white fur, held David at bay. Muscles struggling to hold back the massive beast while still reforming, he trembled with the effort.

Jasmine took the opportunity to haul Cassandra to her feet and push her out of the scuffle.

David's wolf snarled, and his massive jaws filled with dangerously sharp canines snapped at Richard's arms.

Richard only let go long enough to finish his transformation. A brilliant white wolf, with a dusting of grey at his muzzle, he was nearly as large as David, but clearly no less dangerous.

David took his opportunity to strike at the newly transformed wolf, aiming for the delicate area under his neck, but Richard was quick. He recovered and immediately he dove back into the fight, turning his own sharp teeth on his Alpha.

They kicked up clouds of dust as they tumbled and went round and round, taking nips where they could and lunging fully at each other when any bit of underbelly might be exposed.

Ace and Jay released Giselle and they, along with Di and Taylor, backed away, pushing into where the Thrace pack had been sitting.

Nathaniel took his eyes off of the fight only long enough to send a disappointed growl at his son as they all took refuge from the fight.

The dust and sand being kicked up was so thick it caught in Giselle's throat. She choked and coughed, but refused to take her eyes away from the two wolves.

Richard had shocked them all taking on his leader as he had; when a challenge was made to an Alpha, the fight was to the death.

His white coat revealed splotches of blood, though Giselle couldn't be certain whose it truly was.

Richard dove at David, snarling and snapping his jaw, connecting with the back of his neck. He took hold and jerked David's neck, ripping out fur and coating his muzzle in blood.

Not a yelp of pain came from the Alpha wolf; if anything, it made him more volatile and his movements faster and more unpredictable. He turned on Richard so quickly the white wolf lost his grip and slid a few inches in the dirt. David took his chance and snapped wildly, taking out hair from Richard's tail.

Richard turned on his paws quickly and reared up, looking more bear than wolf.

David rose to the challenge and sprinted forward. He collided with Richard, causing him to tumble backwards. Dust kicked up heavy again, and when Giselle could see, Richard was on his back with David towering over him.

Oh no! She looked away, not wanting to see David tear out his throat but couldn't help herself and took one final peek.

Richard had his back paws up, kicking as hard as he could while attempting to twist away from David's massive jaws. One of his paws connected and shoved David sideways.

Richard jumped to his feet again, diving at David's back leg. He bit down hard and jerked his neck sideway.

Bones cracked.

David finally let out a true yelp of pain.

Whether Richard heard it or not didn't matter; this was a fight to the end, and now that David was seriously injured, he was going in for the kill.

This Giselle couldn't see. When she turned away this time, she didn't allow herself to look back despite the curiosity at the horrible sounds David was making.

And then he went silent.

The crowd gasped around her, and now she had to see.

David was gone, but the smell of burning hair stung her nose, telling her where he'd been sent.

Part of her felt sadness. He had been a relative, after all. Angry and confused and overconfident in his own power, but he could have been someone worth getting to know under better circumstances.

Ace and Jay lowered their heads respectfully, but kept their eyes on the fire.

Richard shifted back to his human form. He limped over to where David had been sitting and retrieved a bag from under his chair.

No one spoke. No one dared even cough. All eyes were on the fire. Huge flames grew even larger with new fuel to burn, and though she could not make out his body, Giselle knew he was there. She sent a silent wish up that he would find peace.

Richard, now dressed in fresh clothes, returned to the edge of the fire. He whispered something into the flames and then turned, eyes on Giselle.

"My duty is to enforce the laws of my people. A vote was cast for her innocence. David went against that vote. I could not allow him to break the law for his own means. As is our law, he who defeats the Alpha will take his place. This is not my desire."

"Why is he looking at me?" Giselle whispered.

Jay leaned into Giselle's ear, "Cassandra's testimony proves you're Orion's daughter. He abdicated, giving David his role. David's dead, and there is no contest for the title, so it falls back. I guess technically, you're next in line."

"Oh, hell no!" Giselle said, louder than she'd meant to.

Richard held his hand out, as if asking Giselle forward.

Giselle shook her head, standing her ground. "Nope. Not me. Ace and Jay have claim to that title, and they're older, so let them fight it out."

Richard laughed. "I'm not offering to fight you for your title."

"I don't want it," Giselle said. "I'm not the right girl for the job. And I'm still a kid."

Laughter erupted around the bonfire.

"That you are. One who would need a regent to manage things until you were of age," Richard said.

"If my father truly abdicated his claim to the title, he did it for a reason; but most importantly, I really don't want it. I've been a lone wolf all my life. I'm not fit to lead."

Richard laughed again. "This from the girl who defied her parents, and brought her own pack to fight us?"

Shocked by the truth of what he'd said, Giselle looked at the friends and family who'd stepped up to help her in a cause they had no stake in. Asher, Damien, even Di and Taylor didn't have to come to her aid; they'd wanted to because they believed in her. "We didn't do all that much fighting."

"Not the point. You inspired them. With the right grooming, you could be a very good leader."

Giselle anxiously stepped forward into the circle. "Do I have to leave here?"

"Not necessarily." Richard shook his head. "The Regional Alpha must only live within their territory."

"And who would act as regent while I'm waiting to come of age?" Giselle asked.

"Whoever you appoint. Your guardian, perhaps." Richard glanced over toward Martina.

Numb, confused, and kind of excited at the same time, Giselle couldn't find the right words to say, ultimately resorting to a sigh of, "Fine."

Richard pulled her forward and made her face the crowd of wolves and witches. "Does anyone here dispute this girl's claim as daughter of Orion Silverman?"

Nathaniel looked as if he wanted too, but he held his tongue. His pack of boys, including Asher, had goofy grins plastered across their face, and Giselle wondered what boyish thoughts they were thinking. She might take on the role of Alpha, but she wasn't about to start thinking of raising future generations of leaders with any of them.

Martina beamed with pride. Gavin by her side had a knowing sort of look about him, as if he'd expected greatness from her and was now basking in the glory of being right.

Taylor looked as if the green-eyed monster had gotten hold of her. She'd smooth things over with her sister later. After all, any leader worth anything needed a council, and who better than her sisters?

Meanwhile, Di appeared to be genuinely happy at how things turned out. That surprised her most of all. They butted heads on so many things that she'd expect a challenge of some kind, but no, Di actually looked pleased.

Damien walked slowly over to his coven as if hoping he'd avoid being seen. This new appointment to Alpha meant they would have to split up. Maybe not today, maybe not tomorrow, but somewhere down the line it would become an issue.

She'd deal with that when it came time; there were still other matters to figure out.

Richard placed his hands on her shoulders, giving her a little squeeze of reassurance. "I will remain here as your loyal guard, if you so choose."

Giselle turned her head. "I couldn't make you do that. I'm sure you have a family and life—"

"My life is the protection of the Alpha and the enforcement of law. Think of me as checks and balances. You've studied government, have you not?"

Giselle snorted. Even here in the middle of the desert, she was being schooled. "Yeah. Okay."

Richard gave her one more squeeze on the shoulder and let go. "As there has been no contestation, Giselle will be named Regional Alpha of the Pacific."

Applause erupted around her.

"What do I do now?" Giselle asked.

"Enjoy the moment. The formalities will come later. And there will be plenty of those. It's not all kissing babies and shaking hands." Richard gave her a sly wink. Despite what had just transpired, he looked almost friendly now, like a wise old grandfather, though of course the truth was that he was deadly and fully capable of being the enforcer he promised to be.

Giselle took in a deep breath. *Of course it wouldn't be. Where would the fun be in that?*

"Go and be with your family now, while I deal with the unpleasantness."

Giselle glanced over to the witches. Cassandra's restraints were being released. "I have something to do first." She took a step toward the witches.

"Cassandra's innocence in our matters has been confirmed, but she has her own people to deal with, and we cannot interfere in that." Richard's tone held a warning, and after what she'd just seen, Giselle was not about to ignore it.

"I just want to talk with her. I have no intention of messing with them."

The witch coven watched her as she approached. Giselle walked straight to Jasmine rather than Cassandra, attempting to be respectful of their leadership. No way in hell was she going to end up like David for flaunting authority. "May I speak with Cassandra for a moment?"

Jasmine lowered her head in more of a bow than a nod. "Thank you for asking. Yes." She stepped aside and Cassandra came into view.

Among all the other scents floating in the air, and the horrid smell of burning hair, that odd scent of false wolf stuck in her nose.

"Thank you," Cassandra said, eyes always seeming to be filled with tears. "You have saved me, and... I just can't..." she sobbed between words.

"How and why are still a mystery, but I sensed it right from the start – that you weren't evil. I had to figure out the rest. But what I can't figure out is your perfume."

Her question shocked the sob straight out of Cassandra's throat. "I'm not wearing perfume."

"Please don't take this the wrong way, but you smell like a wolf, but not. It's been sort of driving me crazy every time you're close."

"Your father used to say something like that." Cassandra's eyes brightened, as if a cloud of misery had been lifted. "Maybe it's because of what we did

– joining of body and soul with another, even for a short time, is bound to leave traces."

"So what does that mean for us? Are we truly family?" Giselle asked.

"In part, yes. You show some of my features. The color of your hair. The freckles. But you also have quite a lot of wolf in you. I might not have carried you or endured the labor to bring you earthside, but I am part of where you come from. I hope that's enough."

Giselle stood thinking on it for a moment, looking at Cassandra's face. "Yeah. That's enough." She reached out and hugged Cassandra, pulling her in tightly as if to fit seventeen years of missed hugs into this one embrace.

Finally, after all this time, she'd learned why she'd been sent away. She had not been discarded. She hadn't been some unwanted thing. She wasn't some kind of freak of nature. She'd found the connection to her birth. A mother who had wanted nothing more than family and love.

Tears were never her thing, but emotion overtook her. Giselle's eyes burned as she tried to fight them back, but it was no use.

All this time she'd wanted a mother, and now she had two, and couldn't be happier.

But then, Cassandra was still in trouble with the witches.

She pulled back from the hug, finding Cassandra's face just as tearstained as her own. "What will your fate be with the coven?"

Cassandra wiped her nose on her sleeve. Sniffling, she shook her head. "I don't know. I have no magic, so I'm useless as it is. Jasmine will decided soon, I'm sure. But please, I've just found my daughter. Can we save the unpleasantness for another day?"

"Not if it means I'll lose you again." Giselle cast a quick glance toward Richard, who remained by the fire and returned her glare with a silent reminder of his warning.

"My life is not in danger, Giselle. Don't do anything more. I'm safe. But you are now bound by pack laws not to interfere."

"Yes, Mother," Giselle said, with all the teenage snark she could muster.

"My first day as a mom and already I'm getting attitude," Cassandra replied with a laugh.

"Let me introduce you to Martina. My other mom," Giselle said.

"There will be plenty of time for that later. I have to remain with the coven until sentencing is passed."

Those words struck Giselle straight through the heart, but she was helpless to do anything about it. With a heavy sigh, she agreed, and left Cassandra to return to her people.

28

"Elle, wait!" Damien called after her as she started to walk away.

Giselle wiped away the remaining tears before facing him. "Thanks for all your help." She genuinely meant it, and expected to see defeat in his eyes, knowing what their fate would be now that she was to become the Alpha.

She didn't, however, expect the strength of his grip as he took hold of her, or the passion in his lips. Damien kissed her with all the desire of a man willing to go to the ends of the earth to win back his love. His apology was punctuated by the gentle flick of his tongue. Their lips sealed a pact and promise to fight for a future.

When he pulled back, she saw truth in his eyes: the love for her.

"I know we're not the same. But we have a future, despite what happened in the past. Give us a second chance. I promise we can manage our differences." The sincerity in Damien's voice had her wanting so badly to say yes. But she couldn't give him that answer just yet. So many changes had happened in such a short time. She needed time to really consider things, especially if she was to be any kind of good leader in the future.

"This isn't something we have to do right now. Let that be a good enough answer for today."

It wasn't the answer Damien wanted; that much she could see in his eyes. He leaned in and pecked her on the cheek. "Of course. Go and take care of business." He slowly turned and walked back to his people.

Their future depended on their actions, not pack rules. And she hoped he understood that. As Alpha, she'd be bound to the laws of her people, but her heart would only belong to someone truthful and honest, who deserved it.

Martina welcomed her back to the pack with open arms, and Giselle accepted the hug with all the desperation of a little child who'd skinned her knee.

"I hope you know, when you get home, you're grounded... forever," Martina whispered in her ear, as she stroked Giselle's hair.

Giselle laughed and started crying again all at the same time. "You can't ground me. I'm the Alpha."

"Oh. Alpha or no, your furry little butt will be home every night of the week." Martina sounded more relieved than angry, but the threat was real.

"I should have expected that." Giselle pulled away from the hug and looked to Martina and then Gavin. "I screwed up, but it was for a good cause."

Gavin sighed. "I knew you'd be trouble from the moment you came to live with us. But I am glad you use your powers for good rather than evil."

"So you'll convince Martina to have my sentence commuted to maybe just weekdays, with weekends off for good behavior?"

"Do you know what good behavior is?" Gavin laughed.

"Kissing up to my awesome wolf-dad and mom and maybe doing dishes occasionally?" Giselle flashed her best sweet and innocent grin.

"We will see," Martina said.

"At least let Di and Taylor off the hook. They were just helping me," Giselle pleaded.

"They were instructed to stay home. We can't just ignore the fact they broke the rules. Part of growing up, dear, is learning that every action, even good intentioned ones, have repercussions." Martina said.

"Okay," Giselle sighed. She spotted the girls talking with Ace and Jay.

The twins looked destroyed, on the verge of tears; and Di with the help of Taylor were doing their best to cheer them up.

"What's going to happen to the guys?" Giselle asked.

Martina responded. "They'll go back home. They have a mother still. And one of them will take over the lead of their pack. The role of Regional Alpha will move down here with you and me."

"Poor guys. I don't even know what to say to them," Giselle said.

"You don't have to say anything. You did not cause this. It's the downside of wolf life – Alpha fights end in death. Let them mourn in their own way," Martina said. "Besides, it looks like the girls have it all well in hand."

"So they're my cousins, huh?" Giselle asked.

"Yes," Martina answered.

"But their name and my father's name is Silverman," Giselle said.

"That's right."

"Then why is my last name Richards?" Giselle asked.

Martina shrugged. "Must have been the name you were given by the first people to take you in."

"So, what happens next?" Giselle asked.

"Nothing tonight. We go home and resume life as usual. But soon, very soon, you'll have to go up north to the previous Alpha's pack and be sworn in and take your official title."

"I'm kind of nervous."

"You should be. Life as you know it is going to get infinitely more complicated," Martina said.

"That's reassuring."

"Don't worry, dear. We'll be here to help you through it all."

"Promise?"

"Yes, honey, you're stuck with us. Lone wolf no more. We're your family. Your pack. And we will always be here for you."

As much as she'd tried to deny it, Martina was right. She was not a lone wolf. Especially now. She had a family. She knew where she came from. She had a father to be proud of. She had two mothers. Two sisters. And two more than capable guys, Asher and Damien, at her beck and call.

No lone wolf could claim that, and without them, she'd have never accomplished all that she had. She needed her friends and family. More than they needed her, probably.

Giselle looked out at all the people who'd come to her aid and further to the families of those people. The packs. The coven. All separate entities but working together. This was the future she had to look forward to – continuing to strengthen this bond and learning to share with and appreciate one another. The weight of that responsibility as Alpha scared her, but knowing she'd already had a part in creating the peace here in Vegas, and through that had built a strong network of friends, helped to make the weight of it more bearable.

She could handle what came next, as long as she had her people standing next to her.

More from Katie Salidas

Be sure to stop by KatieSalidas.com and sign up to the Paranormal Posse Newsletter.
All new subscribers will be sent a FREE ebook.

Autographed Editions of all Katie Salidas books may be purchased at
www.KatieSalidas.com

The Chronicles of the Uprising

Initiation
FREE Prequel to the Chronicles of the Uprising.
The great cataclysm wiped almost all life from the face of planet Earth, but tiny pockets of survivors crawled from the ashes, with only one thought: survival, at any cost. But not all survivors were human. In the new world order being a Vampire is a crime punishable by eternal servitude in the arena as a Gladiator of the Iron Gate. Mira, a newly turned vampire, must prove she has what it takes to survive in the human's world. It's kill or be killed. Immortality is not guaranteed.

Dissension
2015 RONE award Winner for best Paranormal

The great cataclysm wiped almost all life from the face of planet Earth, but tiny pockets of survivors crawled from the ashes, with only one thought: survival, at any cost.

But not all survivors were human.

In the dark, militant society that has risen in the aftermath, vampires, once thought to be mythical, have been assimilated and enslaved. Used for blood sport their lives are allowed to continue only for the entertainment of the masses. Reviled as savages, they are destined to serve out their immortal lives in the arena, as gladiators.

And there is no greater gladiator than Mira: undefeated, uncompromising...and seemingly unbreakable. When an escape attempt leads Mira into the path of Lucian Stavros, the city's Regent, her destiny is changed forever.

Lucian, raised in a culture which both reviles and celebrates the savagery and inhumanity of vampires, finds Mira as intriguing as she is brash. An impulsive decision - to become Mira's patron - changes more than just Lucian's perception about vampire kind. The course of his life is altered in ways he could never have predicted - a life that is suddenly as expendable as hers.

Can Mira prove to Lucian that all is not as it seems? Can Lucian escape centuries of lies, bloodshed, and propaganda to see the truth? Or will the supreme power of the human overlords destroy them both?

Complication

Narrowly escaping death at the hands of the Magistrate, Mira travels west, toward the coast. With three weakened human fugitives accompanying her, she searches for the mythical land of Sanctuary.

After encountering a pack of wolf shifters, headed by the charismatic--and brazen--Stryker, Mira learns that Sanctuary is real after all. Caldera Grove: home of the Otherkin. Hidden in the mouth of a dormant volcano, it has protected its residents from humans since the early days following the great cataclysm. For Mira-- a vampire-- Caldera Grove is a land of peace; an escape from the relentless persecution of the humans who once enslaved her, and an end to the daily struggle and bloodshed of being a gladiator.

For the humans accompanying her, Caldera Grove means death. Humans, greedy and untrustworthy creatures, are destroyed before they can penetrate its borders.

To plead her case for entry into Caldera, Mira must abandon her companions, albeit temporarily, and follow Stryker into the heart of the city. What she finds within Caldera Grove presents her with an unenviable decision between her own desires for freedom and peace, or honor and the human companions who risked it all for her.

Revolution

Peace is an illusion. Blood, violence, and death follow Mira like shadows.

Battle lines have been drawn between human and Otherkin, and a bloody war is on the horizon: one that will end in either a shift in the world's balance of power...or ultimate destruction.

In spite of their strength, powers, and a rage known only by the oppressed, the Otherkin are evenly matched by the superior numbers of the human army. To tip the balance in their favor, the Otherkin need more soldiers - and their only options are the Gladiators of New Haven city.

Mira is sent across enemy lines to recruit any able-bodied vampires to her cause. But what she discovers along the way will blur the lines between friends and enemies. Seeds of doubt weaken Mira's allegiance, and she finds herself torn between the old masters who used her as entertainment and the new ones who consider her as nothing more than a weapon.

As the war draws near, Mira will have to decide what she is truly fighting for.

Transition

Peace is just a breath between battles for Mira. Hardened by slavery and war, she longs for the simpler life, knowing that it might never be hers to enjoy. There is always another battle waiting to be fought, another foe on the horizon. Peace between humans, vampires, and otherkin may be nothing more than a dream, but Mira holds out hope.

It is during this brief respite that Mira is gifted one of her greatest weapons. Though it brings with it memories of a time when she was not so jaded, it also comes with a reminder of terrible pain and loss. Awakening deeply hidden emotions within her, if Mira can use this to her advantage, she'll have a new ally in the next battle to come.

Retribution

Immortality is never guaranteed…

As much as Mira dreams of a simpler existence, blood and violence are her way of life. Former gladiator turned freedom fighter, she has carved a trail from New Haven to Caldera Grove and back, freeing her people, the vampires, from enslavement by the humans.

But with victory almost within reach, a new and powerful enemy emerges. One who'll be satisfied with nothing less than complete subjugation—or destruction—of all supernat-ural beings.

With a secret army of his own, he's more than prepared for any resistance Mira and her patchy rebel forces can offer, and demands their immediate surrender.

Never one to back away from a fight, Mira believes she's ready for anything. But with the battle lines drawn she will be forced to make the ultimate sacrifice.

Kill or be killed.

Annihilation

Death is the easy way out. Still clinging rabidly to power, the Elites spin lies of prejudice and hatred, stoking the fires of war.

The sole driving force toward peace, Mira sacrificed every-thing for the cause. In the end, strong as she was, Mira was never enough.

It will take the strength of many to finish what she started, and every race – Otherkin, human, and vampire – has much to lose in the bloody days ahead.

The only outcomes are peace... or death.

The Immortalis Series

Becoming a vampire is easy. Living with the condition... that's the hard part. Join Alyssa as she stumbles through the world of the "Unnatural."

Carpe Noctem
Newbie vampire Alyssa never asked for this life, but now it's all she has. Rescued from death by Lysander, the aloof and sexy leader of the Peregrinus vampire clan, she's barely cut her teeth before she becomes a target. Kallisto, an ancient and vindictive vampire queen – and Lysander's old mate - wants nothing less than final death for her former lover and his new toy. She's not above letting the Acta Sanctorum, and its greatest vampire hunter, Santino, know exactly where the clan can be found.With no time to mourn her old life, Alyssa's survival depends on her new family. She will have to stand alongside Lysander and fight against two enemies who will stop at nothing to destroy them.

Hunters & Prey
Rule number one: humans and vampires don't co-exist. One is the hunter and one is the prey. Simple, right? Not for newly-turned vampire Alyssa. A surprise confrontation with Santino Vitale, the Acta Sanctorum's most fearsome hunter, sends her fleeing back to the world she once knew, and Fallon, the human friend she's missed more than anything. Now she has some explaining to do. However, that will have to wait. With the Acta Sanctorum hot on their heels, staying alive is more important than educating a human on the finer points of bloodlust.

Pandora's Box

After a few months as a vampire, Alyssa thought she'd learned all she needed to know about the supernatural world. But her confidence is shattered by the delivery of a mysterious package - a Pandora's Box. Seemingly innocuous, the box is in reality an ancient prison, generated by a magic more powerful than anyone in her clan has ever known. But what manner of evil could need such force to contain it? When the box is opened, the sinister creature within is released, and only supernatural blood will satiate its thirst. The clan soon learns how it feels when the hunter becomes the hunted.

Soulstone

It's a desperate time for rookie vampire Alyssa, and her sanity is hanging by a slender thread. Her clan is still reeling from the monumental battle with Aniketos; a battle that claimed the body of Lysander, her sire and lover, and trapped his spirit in a mysterious crystal. A Soulstone. Unfortunately, no amount of magic has been able to release Lysander's spirit, and the stone is starting to fade. Weeks of effort have proved futile. Her clan, the Peregrinus, have all but given up hope. Only Alyssa still believes her lover can be released. In despair, Alyssa begs the help of the local witch coven, and unwittingly exposes the supernaturals of Boston to unwanted attention from the Acta Sanctorum. The Saints converge on the city and begin their cleansing crusade to rid the world of all things "Unnatural." In the middle of an all-out war, but no closer to a solution to the dying stone, Alyssa is left with an unenviable choice: save her mate, or save her clan.

The Immortalis Companion Novellas

Moonlight

Good girls don't wear fur, or fight over men, and they certainly don't run around naked, howling at the moon. But then, no-one ever called Fallon a good girl. As a human unofficially mated to an Alpha werewolf, Fallon is being pressured to "become"…or be gone. Her mate Aiden, the interim leader of the Olde Town Pack, is in a position that demands he either choose a wolf mate…or leave the pack forever. No matter how hot the sex with Fallon is, he can't ignore centuries of tradition. Become a wolf or not. If only the choice were that simple. Fallon's options are further clouded by the overt presence of other females desperate to be the Alpha's mate. And when these bitches get serious, it's not just claws that come out. If Fallon wants to keep her man and take the title she'll have to exert a little dominance of her own.

Dark Salvation

A gathering storm of violence is on the horizon. Whispered threats of the Acta Sanctorum's return have the supernatural world abuzz. Only recently aware of the other world hidden behind our own, Kitara Vanders has barely scratched the surface of what being supernatural truly means. A special woman in her own right, she possesses unique telepathic abilities, gifts that have recently come under the scrutiny of the Acta Sanctorum, a fanatical organization whose mission is to cleanse the world of anything supernatural. Targeted, and marked for death, Kitara's only hope lies with the lethally seductive yet emotionally scarred warrior, Nicholas.

Knowing full well the atrocities the Acta Sanctorum is capable of, Nicholas is all too eager for the battle to begin. Fueled by pain and rage from the loss of his mate, he's itching for a fight, but one thing stands in his way, Kitara: a beautiful dark-haired woman with unique psychic abilities and an unusual link to the Saints. Despite his resolve to remain focused on his mission, a purely physical relationship binds them together in a way neither of them expected. And when her life hangs in the balance, Nicholas finds his own is teetering on the edge too.

About The Author

Las Vegas native, Katie Salidas is a Jill of all trades. Mother to three, Wife to one, and slave to the craft of writing, she tries to do it all, often causing sleep deprivation and many nights passed out at the computer. Author of the Immortalis series, Chronicles of the Uprising, and various other paranormal works; writing is her passion, and she hopes that her passion will bring you hours of entertainment.

Find Katie Salidas online at:
KatieSalidas@gmail.com

Be sure to stop by KatieSalidas.com and sign up to the Paranormal Posse Newsletter.

All new subscribers will be sent a FREE ebook.

Autographed Editions of all Katie Salidas books may be purchased at
www.KatieSalidas.com

http://www.katiesalidas.com/

Facebook
http://www.facebook.com/pages/Katie-Salidas-Author/214780936916

LinkedIn
http://www.linkedin.com/profile?viewProfile=&key=58814031&trk=tab_pro

Twitter
http://twitter.com/QuixoticKatie